MAYBE YOU

MAYBE YOU

MAYBE THIS TIME

JOLIE MOORE

MOORE DIGITAL
MDM MEDIA INC

This edition published by

Moore Digital Media Inc
1125 N Fairfax Avenue
Unit #46071
West Hollywood, CA 90046

Cover Designer: Cover Me Darling
eISBN: 978-1-64414-083-3
ISBN: 978-1-64414-084-0

ALSO BY JOLIE MOORE

ONE

Adonis

"Is that what you're really called?"

Gemma Hart's accented voice shook Adonis Andreis from his thoughts. His grip loosened. He watched the rubber, wood, and hardened steel just miss his steel-reinforced toes. The hammer he'd been holding plunked loudly to the floor. The dent the steel head made in the floor was not insignificant. He closed his eyes in defeat.

Using his now empty hand to massage away the pain that was surely going to gather in his head, he added the depression in the wood to his mental punch list of things he'd have to fix before this job was done. That day couldn't come soon enough.

Before he could get down from the middle rung of his ladder, Gemma reached down, picked up the tool, and handed it to him. The face that looked up to him was all wide eyes and innocence. It was the kind of face that could win awards. It was the face that *had* won two Academy Awards. He'd watched her carefully move the gold statuettes before he'd demolished the sagging particleboard shelving in her den.

Adonis closed his own eyes again, blocking out the clear blue eyes staring up at him guilelessly. Blocking out the slim ankles, one adorned with the little bandage tattoo that had intrigued him from day one. Swatting from his mind the fine silk of her russet hair, the same color as fall leaves in Chicago's autumn.

Employers were off-limits.

Gemma Hart was not only off-limits, but from another planet altogether, and their two species were not meant to interact. Didn't mean he hadn't noticed that she was attractive; cute really, in a spritely leprechaun sort of way. Scratch that, a sexy leprechaun sort of way. But strictly, one hundred percent off limits.

Settling the hammer into a leather loop on his tool belt, he opened his eyes and turned to look at his employer more closely, then regretted it. Leprechaun was not exactly the right comparison. Sexy red-haired siren would have been far more accurate. And more dangerous. He'd never been able to turn down a damsel in need. It had always been his downfall.

"Can I help you?" he asked, looking the curvy redheaded woman up and down to assess the nature of her question, not to satisfy any curiosity about how she looked in a never-before-seen short skirt and tight-fitting tank top.

"Is Adonis your real name?" she asked, jogging his short-term memory.

Right, she'd interrupted him while he was framing out a termite-ridden wall that needed replacing to ask him, not about timelines, or materials, or cost, but to ask about his name. Because that wasn't the first time he'd heard the question. Carefully, he swallowed his sarcastic response, remembering he was finishing out this job as a favor to his dad.

"Yeah, sure. Greek dad," he said by way of explanation. "You met him. Proud man with definite ideas on how the way things should be." He slipped his right hand down to his side, ready to lift the hammer from the leather loop, when she spoke again.

"Is it a hard name to live with?" Her "hard" was posh British accent all the way. Worlds away from his flat Chicago-style A's.

"No harder than any other, I expect," he said. He pulled his gaze from her and turned back toward the exterior wall. "You never noticed this was like cottage cheese?" he asked as he pointed to what used to be two-by-four wall studs. Once he'd removed the plaster, Adonis had wondered what had held up the wall for the last handful of years. The wood, thanks to western subterranean termites, looked like a slice of Swiss cheese, but with a lot more holes.

Gemma looked from him to the wall and back, but didn't answer. For an awkward minute or two, they stood in uncomfortable silence. Then she backed away, eventually turning around and scurrying to wherever she holed up during the day.

This was the most contact they'd had in the three months he'd worked at her house, and there hadn't been one time it was anything less than awkward.

Gemma Hart had to be the weirdest person he'd ever

worked for, and in Southern California, where hippies and actors outnumbered the wildlife, that was saying a lot.

Lifting his hammer, he went back to work. If this wall was the last huge change order, he could get this job done in eight, maybe ten weeks tops. He'd finish framing this back wall today. Tomorrow, he'd scheduled the electrician to rough out outlets for this area and the kitchen. While they were doing that, he could take care of the plumbing himself.

Punching in a final nail, he looked at the plans tacked to an adjoining wall. He had to admit, his dad had done a great job on this one.

His father, Dominic Andreis, had originally taken on the task of renovating Gemma Hart's first floor. But a DVT diagnosis and the prescription of rest had Adonis subbing in to finish the job. If it had been up to him, he'd never taken this job in the first place. The last few times he'd worked for folks in the entertainment industry, it had been a debacle.

Each time, he vowed it would be the last. Then the next one would offer him the equivalent of the gross domestic product of a small country, and he'd been sucked in. Then disaster would ensue. They'd change their mind a thousand times, call him at all times of day and night, but expect the job to be done quickly and perfectly. He delivered then said to himself never again. Too bad he didn't stick to his promises.

When someone's net worth was greater than that of a country like Zimbabwe, he'd discovered that same person had expectations of being treated like royalty. He loved the work, but hated the clients.

Except this one. Gemma Hart never said a damned thing, didn't make a single demand, and when she wasn't hiding, was otherwise very, very weird.

Like now.

Between strikes of the hammer on nails, he heard her come back into the room. Her Irish setter, Granger, was trailing behind her, tracking dust along the floors.

This time he was prepared, and turned around careful to keep his boots firmly on the ladder and the tool in his hand.

"Your dad doing okay?" she asked after a very long pause.

After months on this job, he couldn't hold back from asking the question that had been bothering him, instead of answering hers.

"Do you have a business manager or assistant?"

"Has my management not been paying on time?" she asked, her voice raising an octave with anxiety.

"No, it's not that. Look, most celebrity clients I've worked with have never been around when I'm on the job. I haven't met ninety-nine percent of them. I usually go through a business manager, a personal assistant, or the like. I'm thinking that kind of relationship would make you more comfortable."

Because this woman was a whole new definition of uneasy.

Gemma Hart blushed. Small beads of sweat broke out on her forehead. He couldn't see her hands from his position on the ladder, but he would guess her palms were damp as well, if the unconscious brushing against her butt was any indication.

"I'm not uncomfortable or out of sorts," she said, pulling herself up to full height, which wasn't much. Her accent was full of English-school-headmistress authority.

Adonis batted that thought away as quickly as it had come before it morphed into a most inappropriate fantasy.

"Then you might want to see a doctor," he advised in grave tones.

"Why? I'm perfectly sound."

"Not if you're sweating and stuttering when you talk to the contractor."

"It's your fault if I'm nervous. You're a very intimidating builder."

"I'm here hammering. Minding my own business. In fact, I'll be done with my business all the quicker if you can make yourself scarce."

"Scarce? That's not nice, this is my home," she said as if he'd stormed the moat and breached the gates of her castle.

"Ms. Hart. I've got that. But for a few weeks longer, I'm working on your house. You've hired me to redo much of the first floor, and I plan to finish that. The sooner I do, the quicker we'll both be out of each other's hair."

He turned, again ready to get back to work, but hesitated when he didn't hear the sounds of her shiny leather slippers clip-clopping away or the click of dog nails on wood. Gemma Hart hadn't moved a muscle. He'd already made one mistake while she stood and watched; he wasn't in the mood to make or fix another.

"What?" he asked over his shoulder.

"You were saying you'd be done in a few weeks? What's left to be done?"

Adonis gestured to the wall. No more than a few wood studs held it up. He was starting to seriously wonder if she was touched in the head.

"Going to need a wall here, the kind with drywall and paint, for starters."

"Okay, what else?"

"Your business manager has a punch list. Maybe you can call him and get the latest. Let me know if you've any questions tomorrow."

"Why tomorrow?" she asked, stubbornly immovable. The dog plopped its butt on the floor in solidarity.

"Because," he started with an exaggerated look at his smart watch, "I'm going to be done in about fifteen minutes."

"Why do you leave in the middle of the day?" she asked, her tone accusing, as though he was a teenager cutting high school math, not an honest man doing an honest day's labor.

He tried not to get his back up with her questioning his work ethic. He worked hard, if not harder, than most of the contractors he knew. He actually stayed on every job, making sure everything was right, true, plumb. Most guys at this stage in their careers tossed all the work to subs and only stepped in to do client face time and collect the checks.

"Because I don't like to drive in rush hour traffic," he explained, trying to stay patient with someone who he'd never seen leave the house. The last time she'd probably driven down the PCH and left Malibu, the population of California had been half of what it was today, if her reputation was to be believed.

"Could you get more done if you stayed later?"

"I could. But I've been here since before seven. That's a good eight-hour day and I can pretty much avoid traffic on both ends."

"So, the schedule?" she asked again.

The last word Gemma said sounded like "shed-yule." Took him a full second to translate her English to his English.

"Fine. Let's meet in the kitchen in a minute. I'll bring the binder and we can review the remainder of the work."

He tried to keep his complaining under his breath, but Gemma Hart had gone from recluse to frustrating. All he wanted to do was work and get the job done. The next however long he'd have to spend explaining everything to her would set him back. He'd been planning to get the wall completely framed out today. That left him the choice of staying late and being tired as shit tomorrow morning, or pushing the electrician, Fernando, and his crew out a day or ten, depending on the other contractor's schedule.

Looked like staying late was the best way to go. He unpacked the few tools he'd put in his case and walked through to the half-completed kitchen. She was standing there fiddling with her hair. Red-orange hair she'd always had tied up in a rubber band. Now, it was down in loose waves that framed her face, the rich color standing in stark contrast to her unblemished pale skin. Granger trotted in next.

"Why a redhead would get a red dog..." he muttered.

"Did you say something?"

"No."

Adonis carefully set down his dusty, paint-flecked

notebook on the roughened plywood that would underlay the stone countertops. Gemma stepped close to him. She smelled like some kind of flower, not sweet like a rose, but more like vanilla. It went straight from his brain to somewhere low. It made him want to touch her, lift her hair to see if the tender skin at her neck was just as sweet. He cleared his throat to try to empty his head of the improper thoughts.

"Here's the construction notebook," he said at full volume, wiping debris from the surface. "It's the new one I printed when I took over."

"Yes, that's obvious. Says AA Construction on the cover."

Letting the snarky comment pass him by, he thumbed through the pages until he got to the tab labeled schedule.

"Today's September seventh. The scheduled completion date is November nineteenth. That's the week before Thanksgiving. Want to be out of your hair then, so you can have your new kitchen and open-plan area ready for celebrating with your friends and family."

"What are you doing for Thanksgiving?"

Adonis studiously avoided the inappropriate question. This woman needed boundaries with a capital B.

"So we're in the second week of September here." He ran his finger along the calendar his scheduling software had generated. "We'll get this wall framed and drywall up by the end of this week. Next week, we'll tar the shower pan in time for the end-of-week tile delivery. The tile will go in the powder room, and up for the backsplash in the kitchen. The week after, we'll get your bathtub, sink, and toilet in, and the custom Vermont soapstone sink you want down here. Next, I'll get the stone. Marble will go in the bathroom, the granite down here." He tapped at the wood underlay with his right hand.

"And then?" she interjected when he paused for breath.

"The weeks after that will be cabinets and shelves, here in the kitchen, the bathrooms, and your office. Floors, appliances, and paint are after that. We'll go through the punch list one more time, then I'll be out of your hair and you can eat turkey."

"I don't celebrate Thanksgiving. We don't have that holiday in the UK."

"Oh, okay. Well, either way, I'll be done on the nineteenth. How you celebrate or not is up to you." He made his tone diplomatic. How people chose to spend their holidays or not wasn't his business. He didn't celebrate much either. But even if he'd been thinking it was finally time to go to one of Holly's dinners, he'd skip it. This year, with his sister, Zoe, in town, it was going to be more touch and go than usual.

He'd give his sister a chance to be with the family. They were probably more comfortable with her anyway. He made people uncomfortable. The client standing beside him was a case in point.

Or maybe she kept to herself because she was incredibly shy.

Silently, she studied the notebook as if the secret of the Holy Grail were going to emerge, her pale brow furrowed. Even her eyebrows were orange. Odd. They must have darkened them for the movie posters that had been framed in her office, because he would have noticed something like that.

It was the first time he'd been up close and personal with a redhead. She'd won a completely different genetic lottery than he. Studying those contrasts could make for an interesting night or weekend, not that anything like that would ever happen. There would be no up close and personal examination of every mole and freckle on her body. And there would be no thinking about it either.

He tried to focus on the number of insulation rolls he'd need after the framing was done while he waited for her to formulate questions.

"I can't think of anything to ask you," she said simply, as if questions were expected.

He pulled his mind out of the gutter to respond to her. "Well, if you do, you can e-mail me and I'll be sure to write you back." Computers seemed like an appropriate no-contact method of communication she could appreciate.

"I don't have e-mail. Well, not one that I share. My assistant once copied all of her friends on a holiday card one Boxing Day, and I was overtaken by millions of messages until I closed the account."

He nodded in understanding. Privacy was something he understood all too well.

"So ask me when I'm here, but not while I'm hammering, please." They stood in uncomfortable silence for a long moment. "Well, I need to get this framed out tonight, so I'm going back to work."

She and her dog disappeared to wherever, and he pulled out the last of the holey boards. Lifting the fresh, cured lumber from the floor, he made quick work of reframing the wall. There were enough remaining boards that he could use the old to scribe against the new and measurement was quicker than starting from scratch.

By the time he looked at his watch again, it was past six. There was no chance he'd make a meeting tonight, but it was okay. He hadn't had an urge to drink in years. Had never really had an urge after those first couple of years after the accident.

Bingeing had been his problem, and when the worst night of his life hadn't cured him, hitting rock bottom had.

He packed up his tools for the final time, and was heading toward the door, when he heard the slap of her backless shoes.

This time there was no red-and-white dog wagging its tail wildly. Her skirt seemed shorter than it had been hours ago, and her lips were shiny with gloss. Maybe she did leave the house, or her boyfriend came to her. Looked like she was ready for a hot date in either case.

Surreptitiously, he watched her, wondering whether her date would get to take off the tiny clothes that barely covered her. Whether her lips were as kissable as they seemed.

Getting his straying thoughts back on track, he tipped his head in farewell.

"Goodnight, Ms. Hart. I'll be here early tomorrow to let in Fernando. The electricity will be off for the first couple of hours, so you might want to get everything charged up tonight."

"Can I ask you a question?"

He tried to dispense with some of the awkwardness.

"Just ask the question. You don't have to ask to ask me. Okay?"

She nodded, then bit her plump pink lips together, silent as a grave.

He looked at the ceiling, willing God or someone to give him the strength to ignore what couldn't have been a blatant invitation. She obviously had a date, and he needed to make himself scarce before it became awkward. He hadn't seen anyone of the male persuasion around, except the dog, Granger, but that didn't mean the guy wasn't ten minutes out. Gemma Hart wasn't a flirt, so he needed to get going before the other guy showed up. He wasn't the best poker player and didn't want her boyfriend noticing that her contractor thought his employer was hot.

Speaking of hot, how was it he hadn't noticed the strong, firm legs the skirt had revealed?

He pulled his mind from the gutter once again.

She skimmed her hand along the front of her tank. Someone needed to tell her that parading around half naked wasn't wise. With her hand fiddling along the hem of her skirt, she finally stuttered out part of the question.

"So, I was wondering…"

"Yes, Ms. Hart?" He did nothing to hide his impatience. He wanted to get home and get his mind off Gemma Hart. A cool shower, an ice-cold pop, and an action movie were just what the doctor ordered. But to get to that, he had to battle through an hour of traffic ahead of him, all the while trying to keep his mind off what was suddenly on display.

"Would you be willing to have a shag?"

TWO

Gemma

Well, that had gone all wrong. The builder was looking at her like she'd asked to eat his firstborn child for tea.

The tall, blond Greek god stared at her. His brow furrowed. His green eyes were unblinking. "Did you just proposition me?"

"I think so," she whispered, very much regretting that she hadn't quite worked up how to do it right so that there was no question as to her intentions.

"I can't have your e-mail address. But you want me to have sex with you?" His voice was annoyance, not acquiescence.

What had gone wrong? Not minutes ago, she could have sworn to baby Jesus that he was looking at her legs, chest, lips, and having all sorts of dirty thoughts. It had taken three outfit changes before she'd hit on the right combination that appeared to push his buttons. Now... now, he was making it complicated.

"When you put it like that..."

"That's exactly how *you* put it not minutes ago. So what I'm going to do is leave before I say anything either of us would regret."

He was leaving. He hadn't said yes. She'd fully expected him to say yes. She'd changed the sheets, gargled with mouthwash, spritzed with the Jersey Chanel she'd picked up in Paris. Lavender was supposed to lure men in like a siren's call.

Gemma looked down to make sure she'd followed the checklist she'd written out earlier that morning. Patted her head.

Hair unbound from grubby elastic. Check.

Short skirt. Check.

Singlet with built-in push-up bra. Check.

Cleavage reveal. Check.

Anklet snapped in place. Check.

She licked her lips. Raspberry gloss in place. Check.

It had all been done right.

Quickening her steps, she followed him through the dust and around the lumber and drywall littering the floor, all the while talking to his very broad back.

"According to every sex advice column on the Internet, you were supposed to say yes."

He turned, his eyes neither friendly nor warm. She'd seen both in the last weeks. Who knew green eyes could be so cold.

"I'm not a stud for hire." Each word hit her like a bullet. Americans and their damned gun culture.

"Sorry. I didn't think you had a partner or anything. You've never called or messaged anyone on your mobile."

"I don't take personal calls on the job. This is my job, Ms. Hart, not a bachelor farm."

"You can call me by my Christian name, you know," she said trying to put him at ease. She should have said that earlier. Maybe all those weeks ago when she'd first met him. Everyone in California used first names except Adonis and his father. They'd been oddly formal. She looked him up and down, zeroing in finally on the third finger of his left hand. Bare. "Are you available, then?"

"I think you need to figure out appropriate boundaries. Asking your contractor to sleep with you is out of bounds. Now, again. Good night."

"You're leaving?" How had this gone wrong? She was convinced she could get him to say yes if she could just figure out the right words.

Finding the right words had always been the hardest thing in the world for her. She was grateful that other people wrote the words when she worked, when she did publicity on the red carpet, shared anecdotes on a late-night-show couch. But she didn't have a writer for her real life.

Maybe she'd hire one tomorrow. She'd get Sylvester on that. But that didn't help now. Gemma glanced at Adonis when he finally deigned to answer.

"Yes. I'm going home. I'll sleep. Alone. Then I'll be back here in the morning with Fernando to string wire. I suggest you try that out."

"Lay my own wire?"

"Sleep."

"I really thought you'd say yes," she muttered, sounding like a daft parrot to her own ears.

"You said that before. To be one hundred percent clear, Ms. Hart, I'm saying no. I am sure there is no shortage of men in this city who would be happy to oblige. I suggest you call one of them. Now if you'll excuse—"

"But none of them have signed a confidentiality agreement," she said, pleading for him to understand.

"Your sexual partners have to sign an NDA? That's a new kind of foreplay I've never heard of."

"Of course not. That...that's preposterous."

He shrugged on a red corduroy jacket, hefted his toolbox, and without a backward glance, he walked out the front door. She held out hope until she heard the muffled engine noise of his van.

She'd lost a live one. Gemma had thought she'd hooked him, reeled him in, but like a slippery eel, she'd never had him.

Damn. How had she bollocksed this up? It was well and truly buggered. She'd taken out her laptop, and while ignoring the incessant pinging of her e-mail, she'd done the Internet search thing. Resisting the urge to call up her own name and read the latest rumors about herself, she'd instead sought out sex advice.

Straight men were desperate for women.

Go slow.

Use lots of lubricant.

Be considerate.

If Adonis was as considerate in the bedroom as he was out, she'd picked a winner. He was careful with every nail and screw, and pipe. Never did he leave a spanner out of place. As a bonus, he was subject to nondisclosure. The perfect candidate. It didn't hurt that he was beyond fit.

Practically lush. But buff Adonis had walked out of her home like his hair was on fire.

Leaving the smell of fresh-cut wood and a bunch of clichés in the sawdust, Gemma click-clacked to her bedroom. She kicked the patent leather mules toward the wall and cursed first in her head, then, realizing she was alone, out loud.

"Bloody hell."

Granger cocked his head, trying to figure out what she was saying.

"Dear dog, I'm going to take off these stupid clothes, then we'll go for walkies on the beach."

At the word "walkies," the dog jumped up and twisted in circles. Five minutes later, he was back with his lead in his mouth. Now in a warm jumper and leggings, she clipped on the leather strip and took the dog out of the house.

She bundled Granger into the car and drove toward the ocean. Maybe she should have bought a house on the water. Driving on the wrong side of the road still freaked her out to this day. Every time a car passed her on the three-mile drive down Corral Canyon Road, she feared for her life. But memories of the year she'd had a rental house down on the Pacific Coast Highway had her gripping the steering wheel in a mixture of white-knuckled fear and relief at maintaining her privacy.

No, no, she'd made the right decision with the house tucked into the cliffs. Never again would she expose herself like that. The floor-to-ceiling windows that had overlooked the ocean had been wonderful…at first. If she could look out, nosey onlookers could peer in. And with

California's strict rules against limiting beach access, she'd spent nine of her twelve-month lease holed up in the back of the house away from the view. With the lights on at night, it gave anyone unobstructed access to peer in on her life. As uninteresting and small as her world had become, there were those who still didn't understand the meaning of the word privacy.

Finding a space along the soft berm near the water, she stepped from the SUV and pulled out the dog. Before she closed the door, however, she added what her manager called a trucker hat to her ensemble. If she hid her trademark ginger hair, most people didn't look twice.

The pounding surf was loud, but not loud enough to drown out the replay of her earlier humiliating exchange with Adonis Andreis. Somewhere along the line, she'd made a misstep.

She unhooked Granger and he rushed in and out of the waves, barking happily at whatever floated on the ocean's surface.

She replayed the whole thing in her head a second time. She'd put on a sexy outfit—at least she thought the slim-fitting vest and short skirt were sexy. She slicked lip gloss along her lips then puffed them in his direction. She'd even added a bright red anklet, drawing attention, she thought, to her bare legs and small ankles. Every director she'd ever worked with had pronounced them one of her finest assets, but Adonis Andreis hadn't been moved.

Not one tiny bit.

Gemma kept walking west, the dog eventually following, until she was treading the familiar ground along

Latigo Shore Drive. She lifted the latch and let herself and Granger through the small gray half-gate. Then she knocked on the whitewashed wood door at number 26522.

Before she'd come to the States, she hadn't seen many addresses above a few hundred. London had so many tiny streets that many houses were in the low numbers. Like so much else in the States, the numbering system confounded her.

"Do you think I have inappropriate boundaries?" she asked Giovanni Mori when his door swung open, revealing the nattily dressed psychologist.

"Did we have an appointment?"

Gemma glanced at her watch for dramatic effect. "Um, no."

"What time is it?"

She looked at her watch again, this time noting where the hands were. "Half seven. What's the time have to do with my question?"

"It's seven thirty on a Wednesday night. You have no appointment, but you're at my home."

"I always see you in your home," she insisted. It's where he had his office. It wasn't like she wandered Malibu knocking on strangers' doors at night.

"When you have an appointment. If someone thinks you've stepped on their boundaries, what you're doing right now qualifies."

Mortification overtook her for the second time in as many hours. "Crap. I'm crap at this. Total and utter fucking crap."

The pity she saw in Giovanni's eyes was hard to take.

"Come on back to the kitchen. I'm finishing up the cooking."

"What's on?" she asked, unclipping Granger. The dog had been here before, though never in the kitchen of the main house. He sniffed his way along the bottom of the cabinets before giving up his search for crumbs and stretching out on the balcony. The sliding glass doors were wide open, so she sat on the stool at the island with her back to the ocean.

"My mother's lasagna."

"Smells grand," she said, hoping he didn't see her mouth water. A home-cooked meal was another thing she missed. Her mother's curries and pastas had been legendary among her friends when she'd still been at school in London.

Without asking, Giovanni pulled two plates from the cupboard. He slid a large square of the casserole on each and poured two glasses of wine.

Gratefully, she took two large gulps of what turned out to be Chianti.

"You said I should start talking to people." She pointed an accusing finger at Giovanni. It was petulant and childish, but she did it anyway.

"Did you? Start talking to people?" Not one to stand on ceremony, Giovanni dug into the lasagna.

"There's a builder up at my house."

"Yes, you've been remodeling for the past couple of months. Complete gut and remodel of the first floor. We talked about you moving out to protect your privacy, but you were fearful of having another rental."

"Right. I did mention that, I guess. Do you remember

that the original builder got sick in the middle of the job? His son came in and took over."

"You were very wary of that change." Diplomatic. There wasn't any other way to describe Giovanni's tone. Did they teach them that at some psychology class at Uni? How to not patronize your clients by sounding diplomatic. That was too long for a textbook. An article to read before graduation maybe.

Patronizing or not, she wasn't going to look for another therapist. Opening up to this one had been hard enough.

She continued, "I'd vetted Dominic Andreis. Sylvester promised me he wasn't a star chaser. Had a solid portfolio."

"We've been through this. He had worked with his dad. Had more work on celebrity projects, right?"

"Okay, well, you've been saying that I need to try to make friends. That you and Sylvester can't be the only people I talk to."

"Don't forget your agent, maybe the housekeeper."

"Okay. Whatever. You, Sylvester, and the rest of the people who work for me."

"What I was saying, Gemma, is that your world cannot be your therapist, your agent, and your business manager. You came to me because—and these are your words— your life wasn't fulfilling. That you realized after the contractor collapsed on your floor and you were afraid to dial nine-one-one, that something was deeply wrong with how you were living your life."

"So you told me I needed to make friends, right? That was one of your keys to a satisfying life."

Giovanni nodded while polishing off his wine and lasagna. Gemma looked down at hers. She'd hardly touched it. But a lifetime of watching every pound made her resistant to food. Wine, she finished, because wine was fat free, and carb free, and on the whole not too many calories.

"Well, I thought I'd try to be friends with the builder," she said.

"Your contractor?"

His diplomatic tone made contractor out to be Jack the Ripper. Maybe Giovanni had failed the compassion part of the course.

"He's in my house every day. Seemed like a good person to start with."

"Go on."

"So...I told him that we should hang out." She covered up the lie with more questions. "That's what you call it here. Hang out, right?"

He nodded sagely. "Sounds reasonable." Sage nodding was another of Giovanni's tricks. Maybe there was a handbook. "Go on."

"But he shut me down. Said that I couldn't buy his companionship."

"That seems overly harsh."

For friendship, probably. Sex on demand. Maybe. She didn't correct the therapist's assumption.

"I think so. Why wouldn't someone want to be my friend? Am I so horrible to spend time with?"

Giovanni didn't answer, posing another question instead. That, in and of itself, was kind of an answer.

"How long has this…contractor…been working in your house?"

"I don't know. Let me think. His dad started in March, maybe right before Good Friday. So maybe Adonis—"

Her therapist's eyebrows shot to his hairline. "That's his name?"

"Yes. I asked him if it was real. He said yes, Greek or something."

"When's the first time you talked to him?"

Gemma shrugged. "Today."

"So you approached a man who's been in your house for five or six months and you wonder why he blew you off?"

"I don't talk to anyone. It was a huge deal for me to ask him about his name."

"I doubt he knew that. Was that your opening gambit?"

"Gambit?" All riddles with Giovanni. It was like parsing out *The Hobbit*, talking with him.

"Did you start by asking him about his name?"

"Well, it is weird. I mean, it's like my mother naming me Jezebel or something." At his frown, she quickly revised, "Maybe Aphrodite or Diane, then?"

"Did you say that last bit?"

"No. That would be horrible." She wasn't a monster. Just private and not used to talking to people.

"So this man, who's been in your house for five or six months, whom you've never ever spoken to, didn't, after you made fun of his name, want to be friends."

"No one uses their real name in L.A. I thought we should start out with real names. I mean, maybe he'd picked Adonis because he used to act or something, or wanted to use AA Construction to be first in the directory."

"You use your real name."

"I was a kid when I started working. I didn't know any better." If she blamed her parents for one thing, it was not using some kind of stage name. It would make it far easier to do anything that required a public record. Establishing a trust and a company to buy a house just for the secrecy was ridiculous.

"I use my real name."

Ack. He was using "reasonable" tone now. So she didn't point out that tabloid reporters weren't combing public records for personal information about psychologists.

Gemma looked around the kitchen. Giovanni hadn't set a third place.

"Where's Robyn?"

"You're changing the subject."

She was. Tired of the poor, pathetic Gemma Hart discussion, she said, "You have food and wine, but no wife."

"She's stuck on set in Simi Valley. Her call time was six in the morning. I thought she'd be home for dinner."

"It's good," she said, scooping up a forkful. She'd learned to take a bit of everything. People got very offended when you didn't eat their food. "I didn't know you could cook."

"Adonis didn't want to be friends. How do you feel about that?"

"Oh God, you're doing the head-shrinker thing. How

do I feel? I feel like a stupid git. I made a huge effort to talk to him and he shot me down."

"Honestly, it does sound a bit unreasonable. But you have to look at it from his point of view."

"Which is?"

"Rich Hollywood actress tries to befriend the little people."

"He's not little. He's probably six foot four and fourteen stone, give or take."

"I'm glad that you were comfortable enough to reach out. Now you have to try it again, on someone new."

"Again?"

"I know you quit school at ten, but do you remember kindergarten or the first few grades?"

She did remember. It was life before. That time when she thought acting was a fun thing to do on the weekends. Life before did include friends, little girls who liked the same things she did.

"I had a couple of friends, I remember. A girl named Chloe had invited me to tea parties. Ellie had the best birthday parties. You think I should hire someone to find them?"

"No. Gemma, I'm not saying that. Your life has diverged from theirs. What I'm saying is that this is only your first time up at bat. Next time you'll hit it out of the park."

"But if you hit it too hard, you'll strike the wicket."

"Gemma Hart." His voice was sharp. It was her cue that some kind of action step was coming. "To make friends, you're going to have to meet more people. There's a book club at the library, cooking classes over at —"

"I can choose my own books and cook—"

"The point, Gemma, is not to learn everything new. The point is expanding your horizons, to meet people, talk to them, socialize, build friendships in the natural way. You've had a lot of experiences in life, working on movie sets, cavorting with famous actors, traveling the world. But while you were doing all that, you were missing out on some of life's basic skills, like making friends."

"I swear I'm bloody ready to give up. Playing opposite Clint Eastwood was easier than this."

"That was make-believe, Gemma. This is real life."

Sometimes she wished her movie life was her real life. In the movies, she'd gone on painful first dates, played the pretty-ugly girl who gets the handsome guy, gone to prom, lost her virginity—twice. In real life, she hadn't done half of those things.

With Adonis Andreis, she'd hoped to kill about five birds with one stone. Not that she would ever admit any of that to Giovanni. Not her oh-so-suave therapist, with his beautiful actress-turned-director wife. What was so easy for everyone else was nearly impossible for her.

"Should I try again?" she asked. Adonis was a live one she wasn't quite ready to let off the hook.

"You're laser focused on this guy like a stalker. Biscotti?"

She took the biscuit and a tiny espresso, nibbling the former and gulping the latter. Then immediately regretted it. Any novice knew not to mix uppers and downers. She'd be up all night at this rate. Damn. Gemma downed the biscuit in three bites, hoping against hope it was some kind of barrier against the effects of caffeine or alcohol, or both.

"He seems nice. I've already humiliated myself, what do I have to lose?"

"Gemma, there are alternatives —"

"Like what, go out? Join a hiking club? There's not one thing that hasn't ended in disaster." Gemma reached into her pocket and pulled out a piece of paper folded into four quarters. She read it to be sure, then glanced up. "Right, you said take someone from my list of acquaintances and build on it. You said yourself my circle is a total of three people with you as one, so I improvised, branched out, took a leap. Now please help me fix it so I don't have to go down this humiliation hole again."

Gemma smiled. It was her most audition-winning, Oscar-accepting, gamine smile, and Giovanni acquiesced.

THREE

Dominic

This had to be the best time of his life, or as near to it as he could remember.

Finally.

Finally, he had all three kids in one city, or close enough. The best part of having Zoe, Nicki, and Adonis in one place was that he could see any of them in less than an hour. The worst part, they had all taken to dropping by. Nicki and Zoe even pretended they were just being friendly and social.

He looked up from the shoe he'd been buffing toward the firm door rattling in its frame.

Social my ass.

He had one little hospital scare and they treated him like he was a half-step from the grave.

Zoe had been happy to see him once a year before he got sick. And after Nicki had Holly and baby Iris, they'd all disappeared into a nuclear family-sized vortex.

It was a surprise to see his oldest son on his doorstep.

Adonis had been the one child he could rely on not to be all up in his business, as the kids say. But here he was, his first-born son, towering over him. Tall kids looking down on the top of his thinning head of hair. It's what he got from marrying that tall Italian girl. Who knew he'd grow giants?

"You've gotta take this job back," his son said without preamble. The kid had never been one for niceties or social graces. The perils of raising kids mostly without a mother. Dominic kept his retort about manners in his mouth. It was way too late for him to parent this one.

"What job?" he asked, scrambling through his memory for some kind of recent handoff. There wasn't any. They hadn't partnered on a project in a couple of years.

"Gemma Hart."

Dominic searched his memory again. The job hadn't been that difficult, from what he could recall. "What? Why? You've got another two months there, tops. What's the problem? Totally straight-up remodel. She's not insisting on new plaster or hand-carved moldings. It's an easy one. Is that it? Too easy for you. I'm hearing that you're in *The Franklin Report* these days." The little purple paperback was the gold standard for celebrity contractors and their equally well-heeled clients.

"It makes homeowners feel better about spending their hard-earned cash when they see their friends and neighbors have already done the same," Adonis said in that marketing speak Dominic had learned to tune out. Good work should be all the reference you needed.

"What's wrong with the job then?"

"She's weird," he said, as if Dominic had forced him on a blind date with the woman.

"Weird? You got this one throwing cash at you." Dominic shifted to the marketing angle that Adonis thought was so all-fire important. "It'll be another celebrity to add to your portfolio. I think the new clients half hire you to get gossip on the previous ones. Throw the words 'non-disclosure agreement' at them, and they'll be eating out of the palm of your hand. But you want to give all that up because she's…weird?"

"That's about the size of it," Adonis said. He stood unmoving. Damned stubborn kids.

"This makes no sense at all. You've been working in and around L.A. for more than a minute. They're all weird in their own way. This is not the seat of Midwestern values, that's for sure. But it's a trade-off for no Chicago winters."

"I think she's maybe into me."

"A lady, interested in you?" Dominic kept his face steady. He didn't want to let on how much that pleased him. With Zoe settled, this last one worried him at night. It wasn't every woman who could take on a man with a past like Adonis'. "How could that be bad? I didn't think she was too hard on the eyes. Redheads aren't my thing, but…"

"Relationships with clients aren't appropriate."

"Since when? You're not her doctor, priest, or lawyer," Dominic said. "Relationships are a bit inappropriate if you have one with every single client. But one in more than a decade probably wouldn't summon the morality police."

"What about those Midwestern values you were talking about?"

"In a few years, you'll have been in California longer than you were in Chicago."

He could tell the kid didn't like hearing that one. Adonis was as much a Californian as half the natives.

"It could mess up our working relationship," Adonis said, tossing up another stupid roadblock. The kid must like the girl more than he wanted to let on. Now this was getting interesting.

"You have one with her? She never said hi or bye more than that first time I came to her house to get keys and the alarm code. That Sylvester guy does all the talking and check writing."

"She tried to talk to me this week. I think she was trying to ask me out on a date."

"You don't know? 'Cause if you can't tell then I've failed as a father," Dominic said. Why couldn't his kids just say yes to someone? Why did they have to have so many damned obstacles? Nicki had thought he wasn't ready until he was. Zoe had wanted to stay abroad even though there wasn't anything keeping her there.

Damned motherless children. Clearly, he had done it all wrong. Raising kids didn't come with do-overs, though. He'd have to help this one as much as he had the last two.

Adonis was still staring at him, hard.

"Will you take Gemma Hart back or not?" he asked, his face was stubbornly set. The nice square jaw that made him the best looking of his kids was rock hard.

"Not. I booked a couple of small things, powder room remodel, new laundry room floor, that kind of thing." He didn't let on that all the work was for his girlfriend, Bridget Becker. Or that it was unpaid. He wasn't in the mood for a lecture from his oldest son. He wanted to be the one doing all the lecturing.

"Dad, you're better than handyman work," Adonis started.

"You kids," he cut in swiftly, cutting off the speech before it started. "I swear to God, I've raised people who don't value an honest day's work. Keeping my hand in the game until I know how things shake out this year."

"What does that mean? You got a clean bill of health."

"I'm not in my thirties. I'm taking some time to see how I feel, okay? No biggie. I like little jobs. It's great to make someone happy without having to sub out to ten different guys and work out the logistics of building out three thousand square feet."

"Fine. Let me know if you need help with any of those. Now back to Gemma Hart."

"Tell you what. I'll come with you on Monday, see what's going on. Think she liked me. Maybe I can smooth any ruffled feathers over there."

The relief on his son's face was palpable. Why were relationships so hard for this generation? Anyone showed a little interest and they all went running for the hills. When did asking someone for a date turn into a case of harassment? In his time, you said yes if you liked the looks of someone. If you didn't, you said no. Easy peasy lemon squeezy.

All the technology, smartphones, dating apps, and his kids were bouncing off the walls when someone expressed interest. Nicki had gone running. Zoe had played it cool.

This one was an avoider. Dominic wanted them all married off sooner rather than later. Well, before he died at least. More than one grandchild would be even better. Maybe Cupid should be his middle name.

He'd make the drive up to Malibu, maybe shoot an arrow or two from his quiver into Adonis and Gemma, then get back to his own life.

"Good. Gotta go," his son said, turning on his heel.

Relieved, Dominic was ready to close the door behind him, not that he didn't love him, but he had a busy Saturday ahead…

Adonis turned back at the last moment, his brow furrowed as if he'd just noticed the world outside his head. "Dad? Where are you going?"

"What do you mean?" Dominic tried to feign casual. After all the years in Los Angeles, he'd mastered traffic, construction business regulations, but not pretending.

"Your shirt is ironed. There's a crease in your pants. No offense, but you only dress up for weddings, christenings, and funerals." Adonis paused for a moment, his brow creased. "Who died? Did someone die?"

"No one died. Sheesh. Can't a man dress nice without getting the third degree?" Dominic deliberately fished the phone they all insisted he carry from his pocket and made a show of looking at it. "Look here at the time. I'm supposed to be up in the Valley. Want to get going before the traffic in Hollywood gets too crazy. Never know when there's going to be some kind of movie premiere blocking half the streets.

"The San Fernando Valley? Who do you know there?"

"I've been in this city for a long time. I know people."

"What people?"

"Don't you have a long drive ahead? You'll want to get up the Ventura Freeway before it's filled with partygoers."

"I'm in no hurry, Dad."

"Well, I am. Scoot. Get out. I love you, but you need to get home. Or you can stop and visit your sister. I can give you her address on Raleigh."

"You're right about that traffic. Better get the show on the road," Adonis said. He was out the door in less than ten seconds flat. Dominic would have timed it if he'd had a stopwatch. Zoe and Adonis were like opposing magnets. When one was within a few miles of the other, they pushed apart.

Before he could dwell more on the sins of the past, he checked himself in the mirror by the front door. Hair smoothed, teeth clean, clothes neat, he beat a hasty retreat to his car before another kid turned up on his doorstep.

❧

"YOU REALLY WANT TO GO OUT?" Bridget Becker asked when Dominic appeared on her doorstep forty-five excruciatingly traffic-filled minutes after Adonis had left.

"No arguments. I've made plans." He looked her up and down. She looked smart in her blue button-down oxford and jeans. As usual, her shoes were studded with sparkly things, just like her jeans. He would never say anything, but despite all her claims to modesty, Bridget liked her bling.

"Let me get my keys and bag then," she said, disappearing into the house. Dominic didn't follow. If they got to talking they'd natter away a good couple of hours before he knew it. Tonight, they didn't have the time.

"You look great," Dominic said as he opened the passenger door for her and helped her into the cab of the pickup. The big van made her seem even smaller than she was.

He levered up to his seat, and wiggled the rearview mirror that didn't need adjusting. In that moment, he was a teenager all over again, not a widower with three grown kids. He was hating this figuring out how to date again. Maybe he was too harsh on the kids. Relating to others was sometimes harder than it needed to be.

"Are you hungry?" he asked for something to say as he eased down to Sherman Way.

"If I've learned anything this summer, Dominic, it's that you like to eat and always have good food. So yes, I skipped lunch." At that exact moment, her stomach growled in solidarity.

Their laughter that filled the cab eased some of his tension. It was just Bridget. They'd been spending time together since she'd been enlisted to babysit him earlier in the spring. They enjoyed each other's company. He wanted more, though. Tonight he was going to lay it all out, but first some kind of ambiance other than mid-century ranch was in order.

For all the traffic and distance, they were at the restaurant on Magnolia in what seemed like an instant. All that much closer to the specter of rejection.

"Where are we?" Bridget leaned forward, squinting through the windshield.

"NoHo arts district, they're calling it."

Even though he knew she'd gripe about the expense, he pulled up to the valet stand rather than circle the block for a free parking space.

"Dominic, I don't mind walking," she protested on cue.

"My treat," he said, handing the keys to the young man in the red vest. "Reservation for two, Andreis," he said to the host standing at the restaurant's courtyard gate.

Nodding, she moved aside and showed them to a candlelit table in a corner of the brick courtyard. He let Bridget get comfortable on the bench that was covered with bright orange and red pillows then sat cattycorner from her. He needed to be able to look her directly in the eyes when he got to what he'd come here to say.

"This is nice," she said appraisingly.

He looked around, trying not to feel old. The rest of the patrons had huge cocktails in front of them. Most were half dressed and half his age.

"Where do you think the rest of their clothes went?" Bridget asked.

"That's exactly what I was thinking," he said. "They've got to be cold, even with these heat lamps."

She looked back at him. He tried out his best smile.

"So what should we order?" She tapped at the extensive menu.

Dominic was happy to leave his reading glasses in his pocket. Taking a cue from his kids, he'd read the menu on the computer in his garage before coming. "It's all tapas… small plates. I say we pick a bunch of things and enjoy ourselves."

He gave the waitress a list of breads, dips, and meats to bring to the table, sounding suave even to his own ears.

Paid to be prepared. Bridget's smile was wide when the waitress came back with drinks in hand.

"What's that?"

"Signal Fire," the waitress said. "I could list everything in it, but taste it."

Bridget sipped modestly at first then took a much bigger sip. "That is really good. Thanks."

"I'm Colette if you need anything," the waitress said, turning on her chunky heels.

After Colette went to talk to diners at another table, Bridget turned to him. "You can pick 'em."

A different server came with a huge tray balanced on one arm, and a fold-out rack in the other hand. Plate after plate filled the table. He let Bridget take a taste of everything before he spoke.

"You're not hungry?" she said into the silence.

"Gotta couple things I want to say, and not with my mouth full," he started.

She dabbed at her mouth and put the folded napkin back in her lap. "Is it about the work on my house? I can't afford—"

"No," he cut her off. "It's not about that at all. We've been...seeing each other all summer. I want you to know that I really enjoy your company."

"I enjoy yours as well, Dominic." She allowed a smile. Bridget didn't smile much. He wanted to make her smile more. More silence followed her simple statement.

God damn.

He hadn't propositioned a woman in years. He couldn't quite figure out what the right thing to say was.

He should have been figuring that out instead of memorizing the restaurant's menu.

"I was thinking, maybe after this play…"

"You bought tickets for a show? You didn't have to."

"I wanted to. Look, I'm not going to beat around the bush. I want us to pursue this…this thing we've got going on between us."

"What does that mean, Dominic? Like date?"

"Yes, Bridget. Exactly that. This is a date. I'm taking you out because I enjoy your company and want to spend more time with you…outside of your house, with me in shop clothes and you cooking."

"Aren't we a little old for this?"

"We are not too old. Maybe we're not young like our kids, but we're not dead. At least I'm not. The last few months with you have made me feel very much alive."

"Okay."

"So after this play, I'm inviting you to spend the night at my place."

"Oh… Oh!" Bridget's second "oh" was loud enough to summon Colette.

"You guys need anything?"

"No, I think we've got it all covered," Dominic said, hoping against hope that he had.

FOUR

Gemma

Gemma ran her hands against the rough-smooth surface of the plasterboard. As juvenile as it was, she'd gone back to hiding in her bedroom the last two days the work crew had been at her house the previous week.

True to his word, Adonis had come with a group of guys who made a whole lot of noise. But before the weekend started, they'd strung wires, laid pipe, and finally installed the wallboard and added some kind of tape and paste. It was like magic, the house looking completely unlivable one day and close to done at the weekend.

Like clockwork, the gate buzzed. She peeked at the camera monitor in its temporary home on the wall of the reception room. It was Dominic in his huge pickup and Adonis behind in his own vehicle.

Well then, she'd have to chuck her plans for today out the window. She couldn't exactly walk starkers through a room, trying to grab the attention of the guy she was trying to shag, with his dad hanging about. Well, maybe she would if she were publicity starved or something. She'd known actresses on their way down the popularity scale to do crazy things like that.

Bloody hell.

Seduction plans abandoned, Gemma hit the round white button that would unlock the gate. It would swing back automatically, and Adonis' taxicab-yellow van would come in after his father's truck. They would park then be in the house, all in less than five minutes.

Bloody hell, again.

Looking down, she saw she was still in the romper she'd pulled from the closet. Whatever. Dominic would just have to live with the peekaboo back. It was more cute than sexy, which, now that she thought about it, might have been her problem from the beginning. She had yet to master sexy. That seemed to be a skill saved for other women.

"Good morning," she said as the men bustled their way in noisily, swinging toolboxes in one hand and lunch in the other. "You look well, Dominic."

"So do you. Don't think I've seen you more than a handful of times, though. To what do I owe this honor?"

Gemma could feel the heat rising up her chest. Her stomach roiled with embarrassment. The first time her manager had introduced him, she'd shaken his hand, then left the room.

She'd talked to Dominic for the second time when he'd collapsed on her floor. The noise of power tools had been persistent for days. Then it had stopped with a loud crash and thud. She'd knelt by his side until he came to and was able to call someone to get him. The son who'd come to get him, a different one from Adonis, had chastised her mightily for not dialing nine-one-one.

"Um, saw two cars coming up the drive. I thought maybe you needed something from me."

Dominic dropped his tools and walked through the downstairs, surveying the work that had been completed in his absence. Silently, she walked behind him and Adonis.

"I guess it's true what they say…" Dominic started.

"What's that?" she asked.

"That graveyards are filled with irreplaceable men. You've done good, kid," Dominic said, appraising his son. Pride shone in his eyes. The warmth between the two was palpable and for a brief moment, she wished some of that would come her way. Adoration that wasn't as fleeting as a movie shoot.

"So…good to see you back." There was nothing else to say. Adonis wasn't alone. She didn't know the first thing about hammering, and continuing to hang about would be awkward.

"Not so fast, Ms. Hart," Dominic said to her retreating back, which was quite naked, an idea that seemed increasingly dumb by the minute. She turned, her eyes bouncing from one man to the other.

"How can I help?" she asked, putting on the face she gave to directors to make them think she was going to be helpful, when in reality, she was going to do the scene her own damned way and make them believe it was their idea.

"Give me a sec," Dominic said, bending to open his hefty toolkit. "Damn, I can't find it."

"What are you looking for, Dad?" Adonis asked, worry in his tone.

"My bow and arrow. Must have left them at home."

Confusion was giving Gemma a headache. This was why she didn't talk to people. They were filled with contradictions. What they said hardly matched what they meant. First, she'd thought it a trait of actors. But the more she got out in the world, the more she realized it was true of almost everyone.

"Are you having me on?" she asked, trying to find the humor. She was starting to think they were somehow making a joke at her expense. Thank Sylvester for non-disclosure agreements. Humiliation was one thing, seeing it posted on the Internet for every troll to comment upon was another.

"Dad, you're being ridiculous. Get up."

She looked over to find Adonis' face flushed a deep red, an altogether rare occurrence.

"What's the joke?" she asked, still not getting it, but starting to feel a bit more uncomfortable with each passing moment. If it were possible to feel more uncomfortable.

Dominic looked between them. "According to the way my mother tells it, I'm a little tall. But my dad said the Italians made him small so he didn't compete with God."

"Dad, you're talking gibberish," Adonis butted in.

Thank goodness he said that. Maybe he was having some other kind of episode. Gemma tried to remember where she'd left her phone. Should she call Sylvester? Giovanni? No, Adonis could take him to the nearest emergency room this time around or he could dial the authorities.

"…or maybe not," Dominic was saying when she tuned back into the conversation. "Anyway, I'm here standing in for Cupid today. My son said you asked him out. I'm here to give both of you a little nudge."

"Asked him out?" That was miles from "have a shag."

Miles.

She looked from one man to the other. The younger one wouldn't meet her eyes. The older was kind and smiley. In the end, she was still confused. Shouldn't the builders be…building something?

"Dad. This is not… I cannot believe you…"

"Let's see. You came to my house on a Saturday night asking me to take this job back. I'm busy, so I couldn't agree to that. But we compromised. I put my other project on hold, and here I am."

"You were—"

"Supposed to what? Be your thirteen-year-old friend? I can do that." Dominic crouched down a bit and made his voice into a false whisper. "I think she likes you. You should ask her out."

"I haven't gone out with anyone in a…while." Adonis' voice was full of hesitation.

He'd tried to back out of the job. Get his dad back on. She wasn't radioactive. Was the idea of being with her so undesirable?

"Then it's time you did. Man wasn't meant to spend life alone." Dominic's face held a self-satisfied smile.

"I…Dominic…Mr. Andreis…" Gemma couldn't figure out what she could say or do to extract herself from this train wreck of a situation. She didn't do drama and here it was, drama with a capital D.

"Ms. Hart. I've got this. You did the heavy lifting. Putting yourself out there. Risking rejection by asking. I'm here to help Adonis learn how to say yes."

"Well. That's lovely. But maybe he doesn't think I'm attractive enough. Gingers aren't everyone's cuppa." She'd been told that more times than she could count. How many times had she been encouraged to go blonde, if not lighter, then when there were more blondes than grains of sand, the advice had been to go darker...definitely darker. Anything but her signature red.

"I'm not sure how we could go out as you always stay in," Adonis said pointedly.

She had to admit, his deflection was pretty powerful.

"I go out." Gemma resisted the urge to stamp her foot. "Granger here goes out every single day for at least one five-mile walk, if not two."

"*Walk* wasn't exactly what you proposed—"

"Would you go on a walk?" she asked quickly, rushing the words out. God knew she didn't want to talk about sex or shagging in front of Adonis' father. She might have appeared nude in front of tens of millions in the English-speaking world in *Entwined Souls*, but she did have some shame.

"If it ends this unproductive discussion that's sucking up time when I could be skim-coating your walls, then yes, I'll agree to a walk."

Dominic leaned down and dramatically snapped his toolbox closed. "Think my work is done here," he said in tones that rivaled DeNiro.

Gemma was too gobsmacked to say anything to Dominic's retreating back. He opened and closed the door.

45

In the silence, she heard his van start, the motor purr as the gate opened, and the clang of iron upon iron as the gate shut.

Then there were two.

Not at all sure what she'd agreed to, Gemma did the only thing that felt right, that came naturally—she stalked to her room.

For the first time in months, her pile of scripts was empty. If Dominic's meddling had done one thing, it had given her the ability to focus. She'd been able to, for once, concentrate on her so-called career.

She'd have to talk to Sylvester or her agent about getting someone to vet the scripts that came through her door. How many times could she read the same story over and over? Innocent woman finds out her husband/boss/best friend isn't who she thought. Innocent woman spends the rest of the movie running from the husband/boss/best friend who was now the bad guy. She'd never been offered the kinds of jobs that Charlize Theron or Hillary Swank got. She could make herself ugly or into a boxer. Anything but a woman in jeopardy.

At least the scripts didn't have too many labor scenes, like last month's pile. Were women past twenty-five reduced to fleeing, crying, or screaming in labor pain? Not for Glenn Close. Not for Meryl Streep. If—and that was a big if—she went back to work, it wasn't going to be six months of looking wan, pale, and scared on some island off the coast of the northwestern United States.

Granger's nose pushed at her hand. Absently she pet him, then patted his flank, the silky smooth fur slipping through her fingers.

She shifted on the bed, adjusting the one-piece so-called playsuit. The romper had been made for standing around and looking cute, not living. Mentally, Gemma started flipping through her limited wardrobe not packed away in boxes. Something warm and stretchy from Lululemon would be perfect for a walk in the Malibu sand.

Before she could reach her chest of drawers, the dog did a spin and groaned audibly. She glanced at the clock on the wall. Half four. Eight hours had passed right by.

Damn, the dog usually went out well before then. She'd have to pull his supper out and then do a walk.

When she left her room, the downstairs was silent. Thank the lord. Tomorrow she'd deal with the mess she'd made in her own house. Tomorrow she'd deal with the son whose father had tried to twist his arm into a date.

Granger ate his kibble in all of twenty-two seconds. Had to be a record. She gathered his lead and snapped it to his collar. She'd drive down to the beach and work out a strategy for tomorrow. A strategy for either back-tracking from her proposition or finding a way to get Adonis to go along with the plan.

Because once and for all, she was ready to shed the yoke of never having taken a lover.

Taking control of her life is what Giovanni prescribed and it was time to get at it. Because she was one hundred percent done with being the thirty-year-old virgin.

The dog was wagging and wiggling furiously by the time she was able to set the alarm and lock the door properly. But there were two vehicles in the driveway, not just one.

Adonis didn't do casual, but it looked like he was trying. He was leaning against the door of his van, sunglasses hiding his eyes.

Her heart accelerated. Her brain flooded with X-rated thoughts. Since she'd made the proposition, she'd spun wild fantasies in her head about what she'd do once he was naked in her bed. The builder, leaning all slouchy against the van's fender, sent her imagination reeling.

"I thought you'd gone," she said dumbly. It was no wonder people thought actors had nothing to say if someone hadn't written it down first.

"I thought I'd stick around for the walk you promised."

"Well. Um. Sure. Get in," she said, opening the back door of the SUV and helping the dog jump in. After Adonis closed the passenger door of her car, she pushed a button on her phone and the car started.

"Did you just start the car with your phone?"

"Sure. Sylvester said it was safer than handing anyone keys they could copy." Sylvester was the only person who didn't laugh about her need for control.

"Have you ever handed anyone the keys?"

"Not yet. I...um...don't go out. But my New Year's resolution was to change that."

"It's September."

Gemma backed out of the gate, careful not to hit anything, then pulled onto the canyon road. "There was an article in *The Guardian* last week that said September is the new New Year's. I'm starting my resolutions now."

FIVE

Adonis

Before she turned onto the main road that would take them away from her house and down toward the ocean, Gemma gave him a single unfiltered glance. She looked at him as if he were a steak and she was starving.

If his father wasn't on the cusp of an AARP membership, he'd have throttled him. He couldn't believe Dominic's little show this morning.

With her eyes glued to the road, he took time to observe her. She was attractive to be sure. But he could see a certain vulnerability under the hardened celebrity shell.

He took a deep breath and tried to see life from her perspective. That effort quickly proved to be fruitless. Theirs wasn't a Venus/Mars gap. It was more like a Mercury/Pluto span.

"Have you ever been to Chicago?" he asked, his mind veering off to an earlier time when his father had embarrassed him.

"Once or twice for publicity. I think once for the premiere of… Hmmm. I think it was *The Absent Girl*. That one was set in that city."

"I grew up there, in Greektown."

"Yes, I could see that. Your accent is a dead ringer for Dennis Farina's."

"When I was thirteen, my dad took me and my best friend, Matt, to Six Flags. We were way excited because he'd promised we could go off by ourselves, even ride the big roller coasters."

"Sounds like fun." She jerked the wheel when a car passed them, though they weren't in danger of crashing. In addition to some people skills, she could really use help with her driving.

"Anyway, we're riding on the expressway. Traffic came to a dead stop on the stretch of highway before the amusement park. So Matt and I are looking in the other cars. Everyone had their windows down. Not like now, where everything's all rolled up and air-conditioned. So we see these really cute girls. Being stupid, I'm sure we poked each other and acted like boys. I think I dared him to say something and he double-dared be back."

"Please tell me this tale doesn't end with mooning."

"Nothing like that," he said as a chuckle escaped. At least she had interacted with teenage boys. "So Dad leans out his window. He shouted 'hey' to the girls in the back seat. They stopped giggling and looked at him—"

A small laugh escaped Gemma, but she was wise enough to cover her mouth and try to hide it.

"He says, 'Hey, my son here would like to take you on the Viper, or maybe the Ferris wheel."

"What did they say?"

"They started laughing again. They didn't say yes or no. Their dad gave us the once-over and zoomed ahead as soon as there was a break in traffic."

Adonis remembered having cringed and ducked where he couldn't be seen, mortified.

"What happened?"

"I hid in every corner of the park where I thought the girls wouldn't see me. I rode the teacups and the kid airplane ride. I did a mean bumper cars that day."

"Did you ever get to ride the Viper thing?"

"Not that day. I was scared to death that their father or uncle or whomever would find me and beat the ever-loving daylights out of us for crushing on the girls."

The feeling was exactly the same today, the setting a little bit different. Not the scared-of-the-big-male-relative part, but the embarrassment-at-his-dad-having-to-set-him-up part.

This time, though, the girl/woman was at his worksite. So he'd done what he should have done in the first damned place and manned up. He'd waited a good hour for her to come down with the dog. A walk had never killed anyone. Time with an attractive woman would be surely worth it in the end. He might not be willing to sleep with her in real life, but he wasn't above fantasizing about her later.

"I'm glad you said yes this time," Gemma said, easing to a stop. "I don't have a dad who will beat the ever-loving daylights out of you. Promise."

Gemma had parked along Malibu Road. The surf roared, louder than he remembered. The strip between the houses and the ocean was suspiciously narrow.

"Where's the beach?" he asked. Cars sped by on one side. Houses with barely an inch to spare between them sat on the other.

She leaned across the car and pulled a big baseball hat and huge aviator sunglasses from the glove compartment. The brush of her warm skin against him sent a little thrill through his body.

It wasn't that she wasn't attractive, 'cause she was one of the most beautiful women on Earth. It wasn't that he didn't want to touch her or talk to her, 'cause God knew he'd love to do both. It was that he was a bad bet all the way around. He'd have to tell her that before she got any ideas in her head that he'd agreed to her cockamamie scheme.

Back in her own seat, while the dog whined softly, she tucked all her hair under the hat and pushed the glasses all the way up her nose. It was as good a disguise as any. If he didn't already know who she was, he wouldn't have given her a second glance.

As she unbuckled her seat belt, Gemma turned his way. She pointed out of his window toward the west.

"Up here. This is it for the beach. It would probably be as wide as Santa Monica if it weren't for the houses on this side of the Pacific Coast Highway. The tide is washing out, though," she said, then opened her door and jumped out of the seat. In a flash, she was over on the passenger side, opening the door for the dog, who leapt out with more enthusiasm than he thought the beach warranted.

"How do you know?"

"How do I know what?"

"That the ocean won't wash *us* out to sea."

She pulled her phone from a pocket in the side of her miniscule shorts. He was amazed anything more than a small person could fit in her clothes. "Surfing app."

A tiny gate, with an even tinier "public beach" sign between two of the houses led them down a path to the sand. He felt ridiculous in leather boots and jeans, but he always did what he promised, especially under duress from his dad.

"You surf?" Now that would be interesting. Maybe she did do something other than rattle around her house all day with her dog.

"No. Of course not," she said, as if it were the most ridiculous activity in the world. "But I don't want to be washed away in the Pacific Ocean either."

After a few minutes of walking at a pretty brisk pace, she unclipped the dog's leash and Granger ran right into the water. He didn't seem to care a lick whether it was cold or salty, polluted or possibly full of sharks.

"Nice dog."

"He is. I really like setters. Plus he's red and white, so he's a little different than the average one of the breed."

"Not your first?"

"My dad has a thing for bird and gun dogs."

"Bird dogs? Gun dogs?" All along he'd mostly thought dogs were just...dogs.

"His purpose was to chase down birds. You know, for hunts. There are bird dogs, and game dogs, and lots of different kinds of weekend hunting dogs."

"This is a British thing?" 'Cause he didn't know any

Americans to make that big a deal about dogs. They were nothing more than household pets.

"Yes. Probably. There's no tradition of a country weekend fox hunt in the States that I know of."

Granger came galloping back, the long white hair on his chest and stomach dripping with sandy water. She wrestled a newfound stick from his mouth and tossed it well into the waves. The little thing she was wearing lifted up, revealing all of her smooth, pale back. Gemma was anything but subtle.

He tried to grapple with this juxtaposition in his mind. On the one hand, she'd been shy and reclusive. Then she appeared half naked and proposed sex.

"Did you really ask me to sleep with you?" he asked, half hoping his question was covered up by the slap of waves against sand and rocks.

"I did."

That shut Adonis up. The last thing he'd expected was an honest and straightforward answer from her. He'd thought that maybe she'd have backtracked from her original proposition. Give him an out. Because he needed an out, otherwise he might take her up on her offer. Somewhere between her driveway and the beach, he'd shifted his thinking. Probably to his cock, but it was a shift nonetheless.

Maybe his dad was right.

Sometimes a man just had to say yes.

It might be the worst idea west of the Mississippi River, but he'd been right about one thing, turning down an attractive, willing woman was as hard as hell. It was getting harder by the moment—the idea, not his cock, he reminded himself as he thrust his hands in his pockets and shifted things down there.

As they walked south, he veered between "why the hell not" and "this is the worst idea ever."

"Why me?" he asked, pausing and turning to her. She hadn't been watching and bumped straight into him.

"Sorry," she said, laying her hands against him to push herself back. Her hands were like twin ice blocks against his shirt. Her arms were pebbled with goose bumps.

"You cold?"

She shrugged. "It's about seventeen degrees out here."

"I thought you said you did this walk every day."

"Not half naked, though. Usually I have on trackies."

"And you're wearing half a shirt and tiny shorts, why?"

"Because I've been trying to grab your attention for a while. If you have to ask, then it isn't working one bit."

"I'm not a good bet," he finally said, laying out the truth. "There are thousands of men out there, who I'm sure are better suited."

"Like who, Adonis? Like who?" Her question held resignation. She said it as though he was her best and last chance at pleasure.

"Movie stars date each other, or rich oil tycoons, shipping magnates, mega billionaires," he said, covering the scope of what he'd seen splashed on tabloids at the supermarket checkout counter.

"Other movie stars are only looking for someone to raise their profiles or make news."

He gave her a disbelieving look.

"Fine, probably not all of them. But I don't want to sift

through men who own more makeup and hair gel than I do while having my privates photographed or my picture splashed on every paper and celebrity website there is. On top of that, billionaires think they can buy you. They think they can buy anyone. Maybe they can. I'm not for sale, though. I don't want to be some man's prize for closing the world's biggest banking merger."

She had to be blind to miss the irony of what she was saying. "And I am?"

"You are what? Please tell me you're not an actor."

"Not an actor, a prize. Win an Academy Award, get the contractor as a swag bonus."

"Look…" Gemma started rubbing her hands vigorously up and down her arms. Her pressed-together lips looked like they were doing everything to keep her teeth from chattering.

"Here. Take this," he said, pulling off his corduroy jacket and handing it over to her.

"I can't."

"This date will end if you don't take it."

"Fine," she said, reluctantly pulling it on. It dwarfed her. Surprisingly, the dark red didn't clash with her hair. The whole thing—the big glasses, the big trucker hat, and the jacket—somehow worked on her. She had the amazing ability to make anything look good.

And the fact that he'd noticed that meant he needed to walk away right now. Take himself down the beach and to her car, get in his own and drive himself back to Ventura, microwave a dinner, grab a root beer, anything…anything to—

"Let's go," he said.

"Granger needs at least five miles, if not more," she said, suddenly stubbornly unmoving.

"This...agreeing to any of this was a mistake," he said, starting to pace on their patch of damp sand. His boots left a series of prints in a tight circle. Made him look like a frantic chicken. He stopped moving. They stood toe to toe.

She turned and watched the tiny red-and-white head bobbing in the surf. Granger ran from the water again. He nosed through seaweed.

"Your dad is cute," she said, watching the dog zigzagging, nose in sand.

"You didn't proposition him."

"Look. This was hard. Really hard for me to do. I don't talk to people a lot. I never have. Not since I was about ten. Arrested development is probably what they'd call it. So I went about this all wrong. But I promised myself, I wouldn't go a single year longer without..."

"Without what?"

"Without knowing the... Bollocks. Crap. I'm utter and total crap."

Gemma walked toward the water and threw the stick for the dog again. Granger ran into the water time and again before he collapsed on the sand.

Gemma flicked her wrist. The dog clearly understood her better than Adonis, because Granger came to all fours and shook. Sand and water flew everywhere, but he did look cleaner than he had moments ago. She unwound the leash from her arm and attached it to the obedient dog's collar.

A glance in his direction was a summons. Like the dog,

he followed her up the beach and into the car without protest.

"You don't worry about sand?" he asked as he watched the dog get comfortable on the plush leather back seat of the luxury SUV.

"It's a car. They have about a million in the lot. Ruin this one. Buy another. I love the dog. I learned never to love something that can't love you back. And no offense to German car manufacturers, but this Mercedes will never love me back."

He shut up then. They were wise words. Maybe being by yourself for hours on end gave a person time to really think about things. Or work on things.

All the time *he'd* spent alone hadn't led him to any good conclusions, though. Just that life sucked. Mistakes couldn't always be smoothed over with good intentions and a few kind words. There were things for which there was no forgiveness from himself, from his family, from those he really hurt. He'd learned to live with that day in and day out. So he knew that for sure.

Now he could add that his van would never love him back.

Great.

They were back in her driveway in minutes. She got out in a flash and opened the back door for the dog. He followed her lead and stood by the SUV watching what was clearly a daily routine. Granger stood stock still on the driveway pavement while Gemma retrieved a towel from a hook next to the garage. Next, she took a hose and sprayed the dog gently. Granger did the shake thing again, then Gemma dried the dog. He rolled, and preened, and groaned under her hands. If she could make a dog that happy…

"You promised yourself what, Gemma Hart?"

Standing, she dropped the towel into a rainbow-colored basket and hung up the hose. The cap and glasses went back into the glove compartment, and she locked the car's doors with a beep.

"I promised myself, Adonis Andreis, that I wouldn't pass my next birthday without finally ridding myself of my virginity."

SIX

Gemma

For the first time in years, she'd said it out loud. From the look of astonishment on Adonis' face, Gemma thought that maybe she should have kept that bit to herself.

Certainly wished she had before Andy O'Bryan had made it his mission to relieve her of her virginity. And make that mission public.

"How..." Adonis' face was all gawping mouth and bewilderment. Not exactly the look she'd been trying to cultivate the last few days. It was miles from the frank admiration and panting arousal she'd hoped for.

"Can we not talk about that right now?" she asked, regretting the new open-and-honest promise she'd made to herself at the beginning of the month.

"When's your birthday?" he pressed.

She should have at least expected that question. Suddenly she wished it was in January, or someday far in the future that she wouldn't have to confront for a long, long while. Well, nothing could change the fact that her parents had holiday sex. Gemma wondered if there were more babies born in September than any other month, in the Christian world at least. She was about to pull the phone from her pocket to ask it when Adonis' hand grazed her cheek, turning her head toward his.

"Gemma?" His eyes locked with hers. Took all her might not to look away at the mountains, the ocean, the horizon, something other than the question in his eyes.

"What?" Her mind stopped whizzing about for a moment and came back to focus on the living, breathing, attractive man standing next to her and the wet dog in her driveway. The truth pressed against her lips, then spilled out. "A week from Saturday."

"Oh."

Gemma took a deep breath. She'd gone this far. "I really don't want to talk about this any longer. If you're not going to do it, let's call it a night." She started to walk toward the keypad next to her front door. She'd punch six digits and be in the safety of her home once again. After a night or twenty of mental self-flagellation, the memory of this very horrible moment would fade and she could figure out some other way to get what she wanted, and what she was starting to think she needed. Human connection.

"I'm no longer saying no."

The deep voice grazed her ears. Her feet stopped moving. Her heart nearly came to a dead halt as well. He didn't say no. He hadn't said no. All was not lost.

Filling her lungs with breath, she turned around to face Adonis. He hadn't moved except to thrust his hands in his pockets. The jeans stretched across his...she looked up at the two-tone button-front shirt that molded to his body like a second skin. Little flecks of plaster or paint dotted the black and red fabric.

"What do I have to do to get you to say yes?" She cursed her mouth, then. Her mouth had decided to forge this path and had gone on ahead without her mind's full consent.

He grabbed the extra fabric of the sleeves of his too-big jacket and pulled her toward him. Gemma took small sips of air, but couldn't seem to get enough in her lungs to breathe.

"Let's see if we're at least compatible," he whispered before his mouth descended to hers.

Her mind whirled around, trying to gain purchase.

Compatible.

What did that mean? What did he mean? How could they not be compatible when she practically melted every time he came near?

Her brain stopped when his lips slipped along hers, slowly at first. Then he slanted his head and the kiss got a little bolder.

Every cell in her body wanted more, wanted to pull him closer, wanted to feel his skin. She lifted her hands and wove them around his neck. Everything in her body tingled, her lips, ears, belly, even her scalp. Suddenly, her decision didn't seem neither stupid nor rash, but the right-est, smartest thing she'd done in a long, long time.

Walking a single step brought their bodies together. Gemma couldn't remember the last time she'd been this close to someone, where she could smell their very essence. Adonis' essence was plaster and paint and sweat mixed with a smell that was all his own.

He pulled his mouth away. There wasn't a second to lodge the protest that nearly passed her lips. His hands were in her hair, tugging lightly. Her head fell back and he opened his hot mouth on her neck.

Wow. That was the only proper word for Adonis and his mouth. Wow. If a kiss could melt her insides, a touch below her neck would set her on fire.

"We need to get inside." His voice was gruff.

Suddenly conscious of the display they were making, Gemma took two giant steps toward the panel, punched in the code, and pushed open the door. For a moment, she worried that the spell had been broken, that he'd stay behind the threshold. But her worry was squashed when he pushed in behind her and Granger, closing the door hard.

Trying not to run, she moved as quickly as possible to her bedroom.

Shutting out the dog, Adonis closed another door.

It was them.

Only them.

And a huge king-size bed raised on a six-inch platform. The room, normally flooded with light, was cast in deep shadows, the sun having dipped close to the horizon. Not able to look at the man she'd invited into her inner sanctum, Gemma tiptoed around him and pushed up the dimmer switch. The sconces on either side of the bed and the tiny halogen spots along the ceiling beam glowed weakly, inadvertently setting the scene for seduction.

"Are the lights... I...um..." What did people say at a time like this? She tried to remember her lines from her last lovemaking scene, but her head was woefully blank. "I don't know what comes next," she blurted.

"What do you want to be next, Gemma?"

In movies, this was always carefully scripted. She'd lost her on-screen virginity twice. "In *Entwined Souls*, I was supposed to be fated. The community elders orchestrated the first time between the boy and girl. In *The Absent Girl*, it was one of those Lolita situations."

"Real life isn't anything like the movies, Gemma. At least it wasn't for me."

She walked over and sat on the bed's gray comforter, kicking off her shoes. "I guess if it were like the movies, then I'd have more experience than I do." She laughed awkwardly.

Adonis fell to one of the orange leather chairs her decorator had insisted upon. He untied first one heavy boot, then the next. He pulled off his socks and tucked them in the collar of the boots. Standing, he took one step, then another toward her. With each step, her heart accelerated.

This was going to happen. Finally, she was going to have something in common with the rest of the world, rather than everything about her life being an anomaly.

Instead of sitting next to her, Adonis knelt before her on the small platform. Gently, he parted her knees and fitted his hips between. Eyes level, she flicked hers away, staring over his shoulder at the black and white spots in the cowhide rug.

She'd made a wish then gotten what she'd fantasized about so many nights, right here in this bed, Adonis Andreis.

"What are you thinking, Gemma? You're not here with me anymore."

"I got my wish, but I don't know what to do with you."

"What feels good?"

Heat rushed to her skin. It was as though sweat was prickling from every single pore. "Kissing you felt good."

He lifted her arms and slipped his jacket from her shoulders. "Then why don't we start there."

His kiss started out as tentative as the last time, as if she were as unsure as a skittish rabbit. She'd made herself a promise. She never shied away from her commitments. So she lifted her hands and grabbed handfuls of his shirt, pulling him ever closer.

Tilting her head, she opened her mouth a bit, wordlessly inviting him to kiss her deeply. His tongue came out in exploration. He tasted like heaven. So much better than tobacco disguised with mint, like she'd experienced on far too many movie sets.

"You taste really good," she said after leaning back. Gemma flattened her hands along his collar, the little flecks of plaster bumpy under her fingers. Slowly, not breaking her stare this time, she unbuttoned first one, then two buttons. When there was no protest from him, she quickly undid the remainder and spread the shirt wide. The reward was more than worth the effort.

A broad, hard chest lay under her exploring fingers. A sprinkling of light brown hair covered his skin. Flat nipples sat along the strong planes of his pecs. As if moving on its own, Gemma's hand followed the tracing of hair that arrowed its way down to his jeans.

His stomach sucked in suddenly as she laid her fingers

against his belt buckle. The double-thick layer of fabric at the zip did little to hide the telltale bulge below.

That was for her. Despite his protests, in spite of who she was, he wanted her.

Taking her hands from him, she reached behind her back and undid the single snap holding her top together. The sleeveless top slipped off her shoulders with the slightest lean forward.

Adonis placed a kiss on the top of her head. His lips moved to the side of her neck, his tongue darting out and leaving a hot, sweet trail. She gasped when his open mouth landed hotly on the sheer lace covering her breast.

Holy Jesus, she would never survive this. This feeling like something was trying to claw its way from her skin.

Pushing his shirt from his shoulders, she grasped his shoulders, bringing them closer.

Seconds later, the scrap of lace that had covered her breasts was nowhere to be found, and they'd gone from vertical to horizontal in the blink of an eye. He lay next to her, his movements lazy and unhurried.

All she wanted was hurry. As in, hurry up and get it over with. Tick the "first time" box and move on. He was anything but in a hurry. Reverently, Adonis smoothed a hand down her body, barely grazing her breast, but pushing the romper off her legs. A tiny black thong was all that remained.

Exposed.

She'd never felt so exposed to a man.

She concentrated on staying still, resisting the urge to push her breasts into his palms, shove her hips toward his.

She curved her hands around the back of his head and

brought it back down. Kissing. That was something she could do.

Gemma had prided herself on always being a fast study. When Adonis lifted his mouth this time, his pupils were dilated; the little green that remained was intensely dark. One thing mastered. While she was trying to figure out what she could do to turn him on, he lay his palm flat against her hard nipple.

When his hand plumped the breast closest to him, she knew he wasn't playing anymore.

"Oh...oh my God," she said when his lips and tongue finally closed around her nipple.

His teeth grazed her flesh as he pulled away in an instant. "Sorry. You okay?"

"Yes. It was just intense. Better than I expected."

His chuckle was mischievous as he bent his head again, this time taking the other nipple deep into his mouth. This time he didn't flinch at her cry of pleasure. He kissed a hot, wet trail back up her chest, taking her lips again.

Her hands made deliberate work of separating the buckle from belt loop. Not able to hold back any longer, she rolled to her side, slipping a leg between the coarse fabric covering his thighs. She let out a moan when the rough of denim brushed against the smooth of silk of her underwear.

One last hurdle flitted to the front of her mind, stopping her from enjoying every smell, touch, taste of the feast before her.

"Do you... God. Do you have a condom? I don't. I can order, but I didn't know...size."

"In my wallet. I usually…"

Gemma disentangled her leg from his. He turned from her, placing his feet on the floor. He lifted his jacket and walked to the en suite.

What would he look like, she wondered. How big, how hard? Would he come out naked, condom rolled on his cock? Would he have it in hand, maybe jerking it when he saw her?

Her body cooled when one minute morphed into two, then five. He didn't seem old enough for a heart attack.

"Adonis?"

He came from the bathroom, pants still buttoned, the buckle that she'd opened was closed, tight.

"I'm sorry, Gemma. I… This is a bad idea. I let my… I shouldn't. I need to get home."

The exposure that had felt sexy a few minutes ago was mortifying now. Awkwardly, she pulled the two sides of the blanket from the bed and fisted the cold fabric up under her chin.

"Oh…okay."

What in the hell else was she supposed to say?

He looked like he was going to hug her or something. She was considering how she was going to feel about some platonic contact versus what she really wanted, when Adonis let out a big yelp. His body came down on the bed with a bounce.

"What happened?"

"Stubbed my toe on this platform."

"Yeah, I used to do that if it was dark. Funnily enough, Granger's never had a problem. You going to be okay?"

"It's fine. Look, Gemma. I should have said no to you

out there. I'm not relationship material right now. I may never be. It's not fair to mix you up in all that."

"I didn't ask for all that, Adonis," she said, mimicking his slang. She wasn't relationship material either. She was enlightened enough to know that at least. One-night stand and relationship were polar opposites. Rather than plead her case, though, she remained silent.

He stood, carefully stepping down this time. He picked up his shirt from the floor, threw it over his broad shoulders. Like a kid new to dressing, he looked down, careful to match button with hole.

With his eyes averted, she extracted pajamas from the throw pillow she used to disguise them. As fast as she could, she pulled on the top and bottom.

There wasn't any reason to keep Granger out, so she stepped down and opened the door. The setter bounded in like he'd been excluded for hours instead of what was probably only a few minutes. Enough time to know that pleasure was possible, but not long enough to gain the carnal knowledge she desperately needed.

After Adonis put on his socks and boots and jacket, he looked at the door like a cat desperate to escape. Smoothing the bedcovers, she sat in the middle, legs crossed, her back propped against the pillows. Granger arranged his head in her lap. Absently, she stroked the dog.

Adonis might have looked like a Greek god, but he didn't look like a man playing games.

"Why aren't you a good bet?"

SEVEN

Adonis

He hadn't answered Gemma's question that night.
Instead, he was sitting in the rec room of a church in
Moorpark, eating stale cookies and drinking even more
stale coffee. He'd spent one very long hour in his van
trying to figure out who gave up sex, with a really hot
celebrity actress, in favor of a roomful of people in recovery. He couldn't make sense of it until the last speaker
rose.

He closed his eyes as the woman told the same tale
others had shared over the years. How their addiction had
robbed them of their autonomy. How men took a woman's
inebriation as a license to violate them. The story sparked
the same outrage in him that it had sparked all those years
ago. Outrage that had fueled his anger and led him down
the path to making the biggest mistake of his life.

As the meeting wound up, Adonis lingered in the back.

"If it isn't the Greek god," Claude Crawford said, clapping him on the back, hard.

"Been a while since I saw you." Adonis grabbed Claude's right hand and shook it.

"Spending more time at home these days. Stacee cooks real good. You should come over sometime."

"Maybe." Adonis meant no, but was trying to be nice. Dinner parties were awkward for everyone around him. When people are drinking, they can never think what to offer a sober person besides water, not that Claude would make that mistake. But it would still be awkward nonetheless. He'd stopped being fit human company years ago.

"We should make a plan. Your maybes never become yeses."

"How's it going with Stacee?" Adonis asked, changing the subject from his lack of social graces.

"Still good. Been four years."

"Mmm-hmmm." He hadn't had any relationship approaching that time. But for some reason he was thinking about it. Maybe it was because his brother and sister had settled down. Maybe it was because Dominic was always going on about it. Either way, he was starting to wonder if his past was really a disqualification for a future.

"Have you told her your rock-bottom stories?" he asked. Claude had a couple of doozies. He'd made a good sponsor because he hadn't judged Adonis when everyone else had.

"What are you doing right now?" Claude asked, looking scarily inspired.

"Going home."

"Wrong answer. You're coming home with me."

"Don't you think you should call Stacee first?"

Claude gave him a look that made him feel like a stray puppy in need of a home, or at least a big bowl of kibble.

Adonis shifted his gaze out the window as they pulled up to the nondescript tan and brown stucco structure that looked no different from the grocery and drug stores across the street. It was like the same builder did all the exteriors and the only difference was the number of bathrooms. But he didn't say any of that to Claude. Ugly stucco notwithstanding, this was a huge step up from Claude living in his car.

"Adonis Andreis. Well aren't you a sight for sore eyes. It's been too long," Stacee said through the open door after the elevator had chimed on arrival. She wrapped him in a bear hug next, not letting go for a good long time.

Human contact. The feeling of being touched by another human being made his head throb behind his eyes and above his nose. Kind of the way he'd felt when he'd escaped to Gemma's bathroom.

He stuffed down the urge to push her away. The warmth and smell of a woman reminded him that he could go a week or two without being touched by another human being. This week had been an overload.

Until this afternoon, he didn't know how much he'd missed it. He couldn't tell Gemma, or Stacee for that matter, how little he deserved it.

"Sorry for barging in on you like this, but Claude here wouldn't take no for an answer."

"You never need to apologize, Adonis. You know what, I take that back," she said, turning into the narrow galley kitchen immediately to the left of the front door.

"You have to tell me why it's taken you all these years to come to my house."

"I didn't want to intrude."

"How is it an intrusion when I extended an invitation?"

"Invitation?"

"Don't go all coy on me. I have your e-mail address. Claude has seen you some nights. I swear... Well, I'm not going to dwell on all that. Just glad to have you here—finally. You eat shrimp?"

"Sure."

"Good. My brother picked this up at the Ventura Harbor fish market. Fresh off the boat. You game?"

"Sure," he repeated as his stomach growled in solidarity.

"You make me laugh, Mr. Adonis. Have a seat in front of that too big television Claude bought."

"I got it so you would watch Food Network," Claude protested in earnest.

"If that's true, what channel is the Food Network?"

"Let me show you the bathrooms, you can give me your opinion on today's construction," Claude said, steering Adonis by the shoulder into the rest of the apartment. The engineered hardwood floors and engineered stone counters were a dead ringer for those in his own apartment. It all looked beautiful on the surface, but when did the imitation of something become a stand-in for the real thing?

"It's beautiful. Gotta beat the nineteen eighty-five F one-fifty."

"Ah, man. I still dream about that car. It was a work-horse and a hell of a temporary house."

"Can't beat a real roof overhead, though."

"True. You bought a house yet?"

"Not in this market. Not ready to mortgage the rest of my life."

"I'm not talking the mini mansion of the moment. But I always thought you'd do a fixer or a flipper or something like that."

"I grew up in a house that wasn't ever finished. I wouldn't do that to myself."

"You seeing anyone?"

Stacee set some plates on the dining table in the open-plan room. "Is that why we haven't seen you? Some girl or...guy taking up all your time?" Her eyes flickered away as if she was embarrassed to have made the wrong assumption.

"No guys," he said to Stacee's retreating back.

A steaming ceramic dish came out next. Stacee, hands covered by a thick towel, placed the dish on the small round table carefully.

"C'mon over. You can check out the TV later. It's sixty inches of nothing to watch."

He heeded her command, his mouth watering at the smell.

"Looks great," he said, folding himself into one of the brown dining chairs.

They joined him. Stacee doled out a heaping portion onto his plate. "There's plenty more, so don't be shy."

There was silence as he shoveled the first few bites

into his mouth. He couldn't recall the last time he'd had shrimp and grits, but it was as good as he remembered.

"You didn't answer the question," Stacee said, looking at him under her lashes as she sipped at a cola. "No guys, but a girl, maybe?"

"A client approached me."

"And…"

"We walked on the beach, but I bailed after that."

"Why? The beach sounds lovely, it gets cold, you wrap her in your arms, next thing you know…"

"It was with her dog, so…"

"Why'd you bail, man?" Claude asked as he got up to get the forgotten pitcher of lemonade off the counter.

"One of the first things you told me was to step back from relationships."

"That was for the first year, maybe a bit more if your personal inventory is complicated. But not forever. No recovery program expects you to go it alone for the rest of your life. That's priesthood, not sobriety."

"I can't imagine anyone would want to get involved once they find out about my background."

"Plenty of sober people have relationships. No one over twenty comes into stuff without a past. Tell him, Stacee."

"I love Claude. He did some shit in his past he isn't proud of, I'm sure. It's not anything I'd share with my mamma even if she asked. But you know what? He's a great guy now."

"Shit." Claude's face colored. "I wasn't fishing."

"It's true. You get up every day. Go to work. Take care of us. Pay taxes. Volunteer to help out those who're coming behind you and need a hand. You're not perfect. Don't go getting your head all swelled up. You spend too much time with that damned TV, and you could stand to lift a broom once in a while."

"Even I sweep," Adonis said, laughing as he high-fived Stacee.

"If I had a shop vac, I'd use that damned thing every day. With the right tools—"

"I could get you one."

"He doesn't need anything like that blowing the fuses in here."

"Fuses? It's not nineteen seventy," Adonis teased.

"Fine. Circuit breakers or panels or whatever. But you're dodging the topic. Why don't you go out with this woman?"

"You sound like my dad. He came to her house and practically put a shotgun to my head, which is how we ended up on that beach walk. But she's a client."

"Bullshit," Stacee coughed into her hand. "You think you aren't worthy. You have that written all over your face. Every addict in a relationship has a rock-bottom story."

Adonis looked at Claude, but the man wouldn't meet his eyes. He'd been a good friend and probably hadn't revealed a thing to Stacee.

"My father forgave me. My sister didn't."

"What could be so bad?" She stood and picked up the plates, their clatter into the sink only slightly louder than his beating heart. "You want dessert? Got strawberry shortcake," she said. Stacee brought a foil-encased pound cake, a bowl of cut strawberries, and a tub of whipped cream to the table. "Honestly, Adonis. You're a great catch. You don't drink, you do beautiful work, and your looks live up to your name. Unless you killed someone, I can't see anything that would make a living, breathing woman stop short."

Claude bowed his shaking head into his hands.

"Oh shit...did you... I didn't mean—"

"It's okay, Stacee. I've come to terms with what I did, but Emily..." He hated that his voice cracked. "But Emily Little won't ever get to have a boyfriend, get married, have children—and neither should I."

EIGHT

Dominic

"Have you thought about what we talked about?" Dominic asked. He was on his knees in Bridget's laundry room, checking on the linoleum he'd installed a few days prior.

"It does look good. Can't believe how much better than in the seventies." She'd shed her ever-present flat fabric shoes for stocking-clad feet. Bridget smoothed her feet over the linoleum near the threshold.

"Lasts longer too. I never thought I'd start suggesting this to people. It's been all stone and wood for the last twenty years—not that you can go wrong with either of those. But for the cost, this is an excellent environmental choice," he said as he used the windowsill to bring himself to standing.

She looked through the laundry room window. "Do you think you'll be able to get the washer and dryer in today?"

The twin appliances were outside in the backyard,

where he'd left them last week. The gray skies cast a pall on the aged white enamel.

He surveyed the work he'd done in the last month. Not too shabby for a man taking it easy. The painting had gone quickly. The new cabinet doors were installed on the original bases.

"Only thing left to do is swap out that light fixture. Then I'll install the appliances. Going to have to get my ladder and dolly…"

"I'll just—"

"Not so fast. You haven't answered my question, Bridget." His voice went from jolly contractor to aggrieved boyfriend in a second. It wasn't his proudest moment.

"Can we talk when you're done?"

Frustration churned in his gut. But he didn't confront her. It wouldn't be right to leave her without a washer and dryer for another day, so he put on a cap and hustled out to his van.

Three hours later, it was done. He'd put in a bright halogen fixture to replace the twenty-watt incandescent. He'd run some rags through the washer and dryer. Both appeared to work without leaks. The brushed-nickel hardware had been installed on the cabinet doors.

Ginger ale in hand, Bridget wandered in.

"This is amazing, Dominic. I only wish I could pay you. I've been doing laundry in near darkness for so many years, I didn't realize… This is just great, is what it is."

"You'll need to decide what you want up there on the window," he said, gesturing to the unadorned wood frame. He'd pulled down grungy blinds as soon as he'd started the project. The cord had been broken and half-cocked blinds made him feel half drunk every time he'd walked into the tiny room.

"I haven't sewn in years, but this is inspiring. Maybe I'll run down to Jo-Ann's. Look at some fabric for curtains."

"There are some nice curtain choices at those big-box stores. Not that I'm against do-it-yourself. Depends on how you want to spend your time." He'd buy the damned curtains himself if it meant they could have a couple of uninterrupted nights together.

"I have lunch ready. If you're up to it." Bridget handed him the pop she'd been gripping. "Nothing fancy. Tuna casserole."

"Bridget?" She turned, standing by the door of the five-foot-by-five-foot space. "We haven't talked about last weekend."

Arms crossed tightly across her chest, Bridget let out a puff of exasperated air. "Why do we have to talk about what we are?"

"Because when we don't, Bridget, I feel like a glorified handyman. One you make lunch for, and bring pop, but not one you can take seriously as a boyfriend."

"We are too old for words like boyfriend and girl-friend." Bridget pursed her lips in such a way that aged her twenty years in a minute. He hated that. He liked making her smile a whole hell of a lot more.

"How about lover? Isn't that what we are, after last weekend? We enjoyed a nice time, dinner was good, that show was funny, then I took you back to my place and made love to you."

The memory brought a warm flush to his body. It was

something he was ready to repeat time and again. No worries about birth control had been sexier than he'd ever thought.

Bridget wiggled like a worm, visibly uncomfortable with his frank talk. "Oh, Dominic, hush."

"Why should I hush? Neither one of us is dead. It was really good between us. You're a hell of a free spirit…"

"Shhh."

"What? We're alone. We're consenting adults. We're single."

"The casserole is getting cold, Dominic."

Sexy siren to shushing schoolteacher. He couldn't wait to get her to take down her hair again. But now wasn't the time to talk about that, she was right.

"Let's eat," he said, following her from the back of the house to the dining room. Once there, he ate while she rambled on a bit about her boys. The youngest wasn't any closer to getting married than when he'd gotten together with his girlfriend, Sophie.

"Ah, that gal's a reincarnated hippie," he said.

"They still live in separate houses," Bridget said, as if having two addresses was a crime against humanity. Damn. Did he sound like that? If he sounded half as naggy, he'd have to dial back the rhetoric when he talked to Adonis. He wasn't pushing marriage and babies…well, not so much. What he wanted was his kid to be happy.

"Maybe the younger generation likes it that way," he said, wishing he could broadcast this discussion to Ryan and Cameron. He could use the points later when they got wind of his relationship with Bridget. "They can have their space and be together. *We're* living separately."

"I worry about Cameron living down south of the ten freeway." Talk of her youngest, Ryan, abandoned, she moved on to her oldest boy, Cameron.

"He's a cop. If anyone should live down there, it's him. He's probably made the whole neighborhood safer. No one wants to mess with the LAPD."

"You're probably right. I think he said something about break-ins in the surrounding few blocks dropping to nearly zero."

"You don't have anything to worry about. Your boys have jobs. They're happy with the women they chose. You did good. The rest of your life is just for you now, you know." He was pretty proud of himself for steering the discussion back to what they needed to talk about...them.

"When do you think you'll finish up the powder room?"

Dominic dropped his fork. The stainless steel clattered noisily on the Fiestaware.

"Can we not talk about this house right now? It survived the Northridge quake. It's not going anywhere. Why can't we talk about us?" Dominic took as deep a breath as his lungs would allow and got ready to lay it on the line.

"I really like you, Bridget. I don't know how else to say this, but I'm falling in love with you. I didn't think I could do that again. I've held a torch for one woman so long, that I didn't think I'd ever find love again. But after these last few months, I know that I want to spend more time with you. I want to go to sleep with you and wake up with you. I want to take you to Europe and feed you a taste of all the different cuisines there. I want you to meet my relatives in Greece. I want to laugh with you and watch our kids make grandbabies. But I can't do that alone. I can't make an us if there's only a me. You've gotta gimme something here, Bridge. Is this all one-sided? I thought after last weekend, we were finally of the same mind. If we're not, I guess you should tell me now."

"About last weekend…"

"Don't, Bridge. Please don't say that last weekend was a mistake. I'm starting to think it's the only right thing I've done in a long time."

Bridget stood and snatched her half-empty plate from the table. She disappeared into the kitchen. The sound of the tap going on full force let him know she wasn't coming back anytime soon.

Even though his appetite wasn't great, he did the polite thing and cleaned his plate, then took it to the kitchen. Bridget had one of those scrubby things in her hand. She was going at the dishes like cheese had been baked into the ceramic. One by one, she jammed things into place on the drain board.

"Dominic, I can't take you pressuring me. We just met in the spring. Now you're talking about…practically moving in together. Even Ryan isn't living with Sophie. Didn't you just say that's the modern way?"

"Sophie and Ryan probably have a good fifty years ahead of them. They can take it slow. That DVT taught me one thing, Bridge, that life is short. When I was lying on Gemma Hart's floor, I wasn't thinking about kitchen remodels, or whether my retirement fund was in order. I was thinking that if I got off that floor in Malibu, I'd start living every day like it could be one of my last. We're not young and we're not old either. I want to enjoy the rest of my days. I'd like you to be part of them."

"About the bathroom—" She pointed toward the powder room that was a mess after demolition.

"Jesus Christ, Bridget! Forget about that damned bathroom. You live here alone. Use the other one. I checked that and it works perfectly fine."

"But..."

"What?"

Then it dawned on him. Like an avalanche of snow on his head, he got it.

"You never...oh God, I'm so stupid." She hadn't regarded him in the same way he'd thought about her.

"Dominic, it's not what you think."

The pain that pierced his heart at that moment must have registered on his face.

"No, Bridget. It's exactly what I think. I was great fun when I was fixing your roof, or your laundry room, or your sink vanity. But you don't need me for the long term. You needed a handyman and I served my purpose. Last weekend was nothing more than payment for services rendered, wasn't it?" God damn. He'd thought at their age, there were no more games to be played.

"Don't think—"

"All these years and I haven't learned a single thing. I think I should go. If you tell me when you're going to brunch with your kids, I'll use the key you gave me. Come by and finish up. Have a nice...night."

The crushing weight of the truth propelled him to his car. He made it all of two blocks before he had to pull over. He was an old guy, with a bit of a spreading middle and thinning hair. How he could have ever thought someone like her would be interested…

Dominic beat himself up all the way over the hill and back home. As he pulled into his own driveway, he was feeling more pragmatic. He'd learned two things today. First, that Bridget wasn't his future. Second, he wanted one. At least he had that.

NINE

Gemma

"Do you remember our discussion on boundaries?" Giovanni asked. He was sitting in his customary spot, an expensive-looking ergonomic chair behind an equally expensive-looking wood desk that would have been at home in the study of her parents' country cottage.

Sinking back into the soft leather of the couch, Gemma rooted around in her mind. "Oh, that night I popped over? Sorry about that. I was feeling down because of Adonis' outright rejection."

"Yes, that's the night. We talked about boundaries. I need to point out that you've shown up again without an appointment." Giovanni's voice sounded nice, but she could hear his chastisement underneath.

She looked at her fingers, studying her cuticles. She was turning into one of those people who turned up like an unwanted sitcom guest. Without the laugh track, it wasn't funny. There wouldn't be a repeat performance.

"Look," Giovanni finally continued. He spread his

hands in supplication or compromise, she couldn't tell which. "I get that you're trying hard to do the work. I think it's important for who you are and who you're trying to become. Maybe we need to increase our sessions to twice a week?"

"It's my birthday. I didn't want to be alone," she admitted. Gemma wasn't such a basket case that she needed two sessions a week. One hour of dissecting what's wrong with Gemma Hart was enough for any week.

"That's a valid feeling, but we talked about this, your loneliness. Have you done any of the things I suggested?"

She couldn't meet his eyes. "I took a walk with the dog and the builder."

"So, he relented from his earlier stance. How was that?"

"Fine," she said, not admitting that Adonis' father had practically forced him into that walk. Nor did she bring up Adonis leaving her—a naked and willing woman—in her bed alone. Instead, she said, "Granger had a good time."

"Did you talk about yourself?"

She shook her head. The modesty of her very English upbringing rebelled against his American ego-centered idea. "I know you said that when you're making friends, you should talk about yourself. I understand your idea about exchanging information. But no one wants to hear what I think. Either they think they already know me, or they think I'm boasting."

"Did your contractor say anything about you bragging?"

"No. His dad is nice, though. He came by to check on the progress."

"Ideally, how would you like to spend your birthday?"

If she knew that, she wouldn't be in Giovanni's office. Gemma scoured her brain for images of an ideal birthday celebration. "In *Sacred Year*, the women got together for birthdays at restaurants or someone made a big meal at their house. Everyone had wine and got a little squiffy. That was fun."

"How would you go about doing that in your real life, Gemma?"

"I have no idea. Feels like I'd be forty before I could meet people, get close to them, have wine. I mean, I couldn't even do it in a restaurant unless I rented out the whole place."

"Do you really think every other actor is hiding in their house?"

"I feel like everyone's whispering, like the walls are closing in on me. That I can't be myself because I don't know what would end up on the Internet."

"What would happen if a video of you laughing and having fun was on the Net?"

"It stops being mine. My memories, my special occasions belong to the world. I've already lost the privacy of my body. I can't lose the rest."

Giovanni's dinner plans cut their discussion short. She collected Granger and went back home. After the dog's shake-and-shower routine, she went inside. The house was as quiet as a tomb.

Determined not to let the night go unmarked, she gathered a bottle of wine from the fridge and brought it and a wineglass to her bedroom. She popped the director's cut of *Sacred Year* into the DVD player and pressed start.

Gemma had always loved the beginning of this movie. It opened like many movies did, using the storytelling device of showing the calm before the storm. Settling back into her pillows, she let the warmth gather in her center and radiate outward. This scene of friends gathering for her character's birthday was her favorite.

Glad she was no longer self-conscious watching herself, she fell into the story of old friends sharing references and laughing at inside jokes. Just as she was about to hit pause—she hated the second half of the movie, where she ran around Fire Island hiding from the husband of her best friend, who was trying to do whatever it took to keep her silent about an ill-timed affair— Granger barked.

Granger never barked.

Not unless there was someone at the door. And there was never anyone at the door.

Panic expanded her heart in her chest. Maybe she needed her CCTV system tied to central monitoring. They'd called it platinum, but it might as well have been called the paranoia package. She'd thought the security firm was overselling her when they'd mentioned the service. But now she wished she'd gone for the whole thing, money and paranoia be damned.

Heaving herself from the bed, and shaking off the dread pooling in her gut, she reluctantly tiptoed downstairs barefoot to the door.

Through the windows, she caught site of a yellow van.

Confusion furrowed her brow. It was Saturday. Sylvester had said that Adonis would only work Saturday on rare occasions, and she would be notified beforehand.

Though now that she thought about it, she'd muted a call from her manager this morning. After talking to her parents, she'd been worn out assuring them that she was okay, and enjoying her special day alone in the vast wilds of North America.

Gemma punched at the keypad. After the beep of confirmation of the right code, there was a whirr and snick as the lock released. She opened the door. The broad chest of Adonis filled the frame.

"What are you doing here?" The question sounded hostile, but it left her mouth too quickly to fix.

"I came to wish you a happy birthday," he said. A single lily and a marrowbone filled his hand.

"Oh, thanks." She took the flower in hand, leaving the severed leg of…what? A deer? A cow? It was odd. Americans were odd, but she didn't ask about the bone. Instead she tried for a more congenial tone; the kind a normal person would have had three minutes earlier. "Do you want to come in?"

Gemma wasn't sure whether or not she wanted Adonis in the house. Rejection wasn't something she wanted to revisit, on her birthday nonetheless. It was too bad proper manners had taken over before she could consider the best way to send him out the door, and avoid minutes of awkward conversation where he reiterated how much he didn't want to have sex with her.

At least he had the good grace to look a little unsure of whether to accept her invitation. He shifted from one boot-clad foot to the other.

"I'm here because it's the only way I can give you your present."

Granger sidled up to Adonis, twitching nose high in the air. Adonis patted the dog on the flank before handing over the bone. The dog took it greedily then trotted off to parts unknown. The only indication the dog was still in the house was the sound of teeth scraping against bone. That would keep the dog occupied for a good hour or more.

"Present?" She twirled the flower, trying to ignore the very phallic-looking yellow stamen. "You didn't have to—"

She stepped back as he pressed forward. His hand came out, fingering her hair before tugging, tilting her head back at a slight angle.

"I don't..." She didn't know what she was negating, but he didn't heed her feeble protest.

Before his lips closed the minute distance between their mouths, he whispered, "Happy birthday."

After last week's disastrous date, she'd pushed the feel of Adonis' kisses far from her mind. She hadn't wanted to remember the heat of his mouth, the insistent pressure of his tongue, or the rough brush of his calloused hand raising gooseflesh along her arm.

The dressing gown she was wearing—if it could be called that—fluttered when his hands cupped her shoulders. It was less dress and more like a stripey silk pillowcase that opened on two sides instead of one. Thoughts of clothes evaporated when he didn't take his mouth from hers immediately.

He slanted his head one way, then another, molding his lips to hers. The kiss went on and on. Any chill she'd felt when first coming to the door was long gone. When his hand moved from her shoulder, through the opening in the silk to her side, fitting between the space that wasn't covered by her bra or knickers, thought and reason returned like a slap in the face.

She pushed him away. Took a giant step backward. Took in and released a lungful of air.

She'd had to learn early on how to process rejection. One lesson she'd understood—above all others she'd yet to comprehend—was that rejection wasn't personal.

"What are you doing here, Adonis? In no uncertain terms, you rejected the idea of any of this. To come here on my birthday with a single flower in hand, snogging me, is...just plain not nice. I don't like mixed messages."

His large hand slicked through his hair, flattening it to the top of his head. Eyes that roamed everywhere finally zeroed in on hers.

"Let me be one hundred percent clear. Unless you say no, and toss me out on my ass, which I'd totally understand, we're going to march upstairs and we're going to make your birthday wish come true."

Involuntarily, her right hand shot up to her mouth to mask her surprise.

"Oh," she blurted out in her regular voice. The second "oh" was an entire octave higher.

"That's exactly the sound I want you making in about forty minutes."

Forty minutes' time could separate her from her virginity. Heat pooled in her belly, between her legs. Her skin felt like it had stretched too tight, as if she would burst from her own chrysalis at any moment.

One minute she'd be this Gemma Hart. The movie it-girl who was really a social outcast. After a metamorphosis of sorts, she'd be a completely different person on the other side of this. A woman whose life included the full range of human experience.

She wanted that.

To emerge.

End the day different than she'd started.

That had been all Gemma had wanted when she'd begun this personal journey of self-discovery. Life discovery. Learning about life behind the camera. A life where her ambitions and choices weren't a distant third to those of megalomaniacal directors and marketing teams.

"Jesus. Don't joke about this," she whispered. She didn't have the wherewithal to do the coitus interruptus thing again.

"I never joke, Gemma." His voice was so solemn, that she knew it had to be true.

What made a man lose his sense of humor? In that moment, she wanted to know that more than she wanted him to be her first. Without the latter, though, she didn't think she had a chance in hell of finding out the former.

She turned her back on him. With mincing, hesitating steps, she traced the same path they had days earlier, only this time the anticipation of what was to come nearly choked the fear from her.

Like last time, Adonis pushed her bedroom door shut with Granger on the other side. This time though, the dog was well and truly occupied. Adonis had made sure of it. The deliberation and planning hit her squarely between the eyes. As sure as she knew her own name, she knew that Adonis wasn't leaving this time.

"What happens now?" she asked. Because she had no

idea. She half wished she had on something that came lower than her ass and didn't completely expose her one side. On the other hand, maybe it was an omen that she was nearly naked. A shrug here, a tug there, and she'd be in her birthday suit.

Gemma couldn't keep the chuckle from escaping her lips. He didn't laugh. Instead, Adonis fitted his hand along her neck, gently tracing her collarbone before lowering to kiss the skin exposed there.

"What makes Gemma Hart laugh?" he whispered against her ultra-sensitive skin.

"I'm going to be as naked as the day I was born, which was ironically today, albeit many, many years ago."

He stepped back, stood tall, and took her in. Despite his admission that he didn't joke, his mouth quirked up the tiniest bit at the corner. Thank God, because they were going to need a little levity.

"Come over here, Gemma." His voice was all husky command and more of a turn-on than she thought something as simple as a human voice ought to be.

Slowly, she put one bare foot in front of the other until they were standing manicured toe to boot-clad toe. For long seconds, he pinned her with his eyes. Despite the rapid heart acceleration that she thought might make her pass out, she wasn't brave enough to look away. They'd kissed before. She could handle this part. His lips would touch hers. Her hands would tremble. Her insides would light on fire. Gemma braced for the onslaught.

"Happy birthday, Gemma Hart," he said before lowering his head with slow and deliberate accuracy.

She thought she was ready.

She thought she was prepared.

She was anything but.

It was as if Adonis had saved up all his mojo for this single moment. This kiss…this meeting of lips and tongue had her grabbing his shoulders for support. Falling down would not be cool, or sexy, or even cute. With a firm hold, she lifted onto her bare toes, trying to gain purchase, trying to keep the fire stoked between them.

Adonis' hand slipped through the open side of her chemise. Heat and goose bumps rose on her skin in equal measure. She shivered as his hand plucked at the clasp of her strapless bra. It gave way, the satin and lace falling to the floor with a whisper.

Stepping back a hair, breaking their seal, she sucked in much-needed air, then trained her eyes on his clothes. She'd been so surprised and overwhelmed back there at the front door, she hadn't noticed more than the piercing green eyes that had held hers.

Now, she fitted her hands against the muscles on his chest, molding her fingers over the blue-green plaid cotton covering them. She slipped her fingers into one button-hole, then the next and the next, until the shirt was undone. Gemma spread the sides wide then placed her mouth on a small freckle nestled in the light sprinkling of hair visible in the deep V of his black vest.

"You taste spicy." And good. Oh so good.

He didn't smile, or laugh, or do more than look at her. The doubts crept in again. Deliberately, she pressed on with clothing removal.

The belt buckle was next. If she got him naked, he couldn't run this time. With no barriers between them, maybe he'd stay. As quickly as she could, with shaking hands, Gemma dispensed with his belt, pulling it from the loops. It fell to the floor at the same moment she'd unbuttoned the top of his jeans.

Unzipping the dark denim was a little harder because he was...hard. It—the part that was supposed to mate with her—seemed so big. She tried to push out of her mind questions about how exactly it would fit inside her, because she wasn't sixteen. She'd seen her fair share of porno flicks. She knew how it all worked...technically.

Adonis reached for her, probably to draw her into an embrace.

As nimble as a nymph, she slipped from his grasp. Before he could reach for her again, she pushed his jeans down to his ankles, then knelt, picking at the laces on his boots. These weren't sturdy brown work boots, but soft navy suede ankle boots. The shoes and socks were off his feet in seconds, followed by the pants.

Except for black trunks, stretched to their outer limits, he was bare before her.

"Gemma, slow down." He took her hands in his and lifted her to her full height.

"Belt and braces. Sorry."

"I'm not sure what you're saying, but there's no reason to be sorry."

"I don't want you to leave this time," Gemma admitted. "It would be a lot harder for you to run out of here naked."

"I'm a man of my word. Here to give you what you asked for."

The flicker of doubt was at risk for turning into a full-blown conflagration. "You have no idea how hard it is for people to say no in this town." She'd heard them all, a thousand euphemisms for telling her she wasn't going to get what she wanted.

"I'm saying yes. Right now. I'm here. Let me," he said as he lifted the silk from her shoulders and head. It fluttered to her floor like a leaf buoyed by wind.

So she let him. Let him walk her back to the bed. Let him smooth down the covers before laying her down on top of them. His heavy weight settled next to her. She tried not to let the heat overtake her, but she couldn't will it away. Instead she was sure she turned as red as a cooked lobster, as his hungry gaze took her in.

She smoothed her thumb against his cheekbone then sifted her fingers through his fine strands of golden hair. It was a bit longer than when he'd started working at her house. The way he styled it set off his perfectly angular features. He might cultivate modesty, but he obviously knew how to enhance his God-given assets when the time came.

"You do look like a Greek god," she said before she could contain herself.

His gravelly laugh was uncomfortable and brief. His eyes strayed to her lips. Unable to stop, she bit her lower lip in anticipation. That single action had him surging against her. His lips came down on hers at the same time he captured her breast in his palm.

Each kiss was brief. He shifted his mouth upon hers this way and that. His hands were nearly as restless. One rough palm and fingers pumped her breast and squeezed. Her nipples lifted into peaks as stiff as pencil rubber.

She strained upward to try to capture his lips fully, pull his heavy weight down upon her, but Adonis wouldn't be moved. Instead, his mouth flitted from her lips to her ears, his tongue tickling the lobe. His mouth left a hot, moist trail down her neck. He blew against the dampness, cooling her skin and curling her toes. It was both good and awful in equal measure. In every erotic video she'd ever seen, there was ten seconds of kissing and stripping, and minutes and minutes of shagging.

"Can you...can we..." *Get to the shagging part* went unsaid.

"Absolutely."

She tried not to weep with relief when his hand left her breast, moved toward her hip. She lifted her bum, and he slipped her knickers down and off. Before she could replicate the action on him, he had moved down to the end of her bed. He rained kisses on her feet, ankles, calves, and then thighs.

Reflexively, she tried to scissor her legs closed as he moved closer to her core. She hadn't expected to move to varsity-level sex on the first go.

"You don't have to —"

"But I want to. So bad, Gemma. Let me."

Oh so gently, he parted her thighs. First, he kissed the hollow between her leg and her sex. Next, his lips moved to the space between her belly button and the hair just below her abdomen. He alternated kisses with sweet puffs of air. As she relaxed, his kisses grew more familiar.

Just when she thought she could take the next onslaught, his tongue parted her folds and gave her the most intimate of kisses. His tongue found the nub of her clitoris, wrenching an involuntary cry from her throat.

"That's it, Gemma. Feel."

Feel she did. Feel restless. Feel both aroused and satiated at the same time. Feel like she was a rag doll unraveling at the seams.

She wanted to scream, so she did. In pleasure or frustration or both. But he didn't stop, not for a second. Then she was weightless. It was like the zero-gravity training she'd done for a movie that had stopped production before filming. She closed her eyes, hoping the action would ground her. Keep her more fully on the bed. The danger of floating away seemed ever present. So close. She was so close to climax. But it was more intense than anything she'd ever achieved on her own with furtive fondling under cover of darkness and goose feathers.

"Oh...oh," she said before she crested the wave.

Adonis retreated, but only a little. His movements became slower, drawing out pleasure until she felt as wrung out as a dishcloth. With a rustle of the duvet, he was next to her again, his head against the pillow next to hers.

When she could muster sufficient strength, she reached her hand in the back of the drawer of her bedside table.

It was time.

Carefully, she extracted a single foil packet. Adonis plucked it from her hand, sliding it somewhere on the bed. When she turned, he was sitting up, his trunks still quite snug, his long legs outstretched along the bed, the golden hair shining in the lamp light.

Mirroring him, she sat up as well. His eyes riveted on her chest as her breasts bobbed with the movement.

"Are you going to take those off?" More than anything, she needed to see that most sensitive part of him.

He closed his eyes for a long moment, the thick lashes throwing shadows across his cheekbones.

The lift of his hips, the quick shove of his fisted hands was so fast, she wouldn't have seen this final disrobing if she hadn't been paying attention with laser focus on what was happening.

"Oh, my. It's...well..."

"Shh, Gemma." Effortlessly he lifted her until she was facing him. Her legs opened to straddle his hips. In seconds, they were millimeters from that final act. Adonis lifted his knees, holding her in place. He held her face between his outsized palms and kissed her again.

She shifted so they were chest against chest, the soft hairs tickling her over-sensitized nipples. The ache she thought he'd soothed rushed back. Her heartbeat appeared to move down low, causing throbbing between her legs again. Without embarrassment, she grabbed his shaft, grinding it against her clit. The heat of him was both pleasure and torment.

When his fingers plucked at her nipples, she nearly shot off his lap. His knees were the only thing that held her firmly in place. Abandoning all decorum, she ground against him as he pinched, rolled, and abraded her nipples.

Breaking the rhythm, Adonis reached for and smoothed on the condom.

"Are you ready?"

"More than."

With that consent, he lifted her by her bum with one hand and guided himself with the other.

This was it.

This was the reason for war and peace and life and death.

Slowly, oh so slowly, she sank onto him.

"How does it feel?"

"Full. Good. Can I move?" Because she wanted to desperately; move that was.

She wrapped her arms as much as she could around his wide shoulders and broad back. With his help and guidance, she moved up and down, first slowly, then quicker as she got the hang of it. The twist in her low belly wasn't as tight as before, but it was as if there was some very deep itch that only he could scratch. She wanted the relief that only he could provide. Adonis was in no hurry though, to scratch that itch. Instead, they rocked back and forth for long minutes.

He unwound her hands from him and gently pushed her back onto the mound of decorative pillows. He shifted until he was above her in the most traditional of positions. He lifted her knees so they were around his hips again. Instinctively, she wrapped her legs around him, locking her ankles.

"That's it, Gemma. Hold on. I'm going to make this a birthday you'll never forget."

Head bowed, he did just that, plunging into her until she was keening out his name. Until her internal muscles were squeezing his cock mercilessly. Until he'd lost all the control he'd kept and was plunging into her again and again until he stopped, a hoarse shout leaving his lips as he shuddered above her.

Grabbing himself at the root, he pulled out and dropped down on the bed next to her.

For a long time, they lay there. The air chilled her damp skin, but she didn't move. Didn't want to break this bond, as tenuous and fragile as the tape holding the wallboard together downstairs.

TEN

Adonis

"Are you going to answer my question?"

His mind skittered through images from the last hour. None of that added up to a question he could remember.

"What do you want to know?" Suddenly he dreaded his own question, because with the most mental clarity he'd had in weeks, he was ninety-nine percent sure he knew what it was going to be. He'd brought it on himself last week, though. Back when he'd promised himself that he wasn't going to sleep with her. When he wasn't going to insert himself into her history as her first-time guy.

"Why aren't you a good bet?"

He threw his forearm over his eyes. The halogen lights strung across fine wire against her ceiling winked out. He could see no more than blackness. It's what he imagined Emily saw in her last seconds. Before she experienced the nothingness of life ending. He wasn't a believer, but for her sake, he hoped there was an afterlife.

"I have to take care of..." He left the rest unsaid as he

got off the bed and went through the pocket door on the opposite side of the room. Slipping the door closed, he disposed of the condom then stood paralyzed. He'd violated his number one and number two rules, by sleeping with a client and by even hinting at his past.

Bracing his hands on the cold marble counter, he stared at his reflection. His life was firmly divided into two equal portions: before and after. Except for his family, there was no bridge between the two worlds. He'd never wanted there to be.

Maybe Claude was right. Maybe his dad was right. It was time to put all of it together. Forgiveness from his sister was one thing. Acceptance from Gemma was another.

Suddenly, for some reason, both seemed equally important.

Unnecessary flushing of the toilet and turning on then off one of the chrome faucets bought him time. Not enough time. If he spent one minute longer, he'd leave Gemma Hart with more of a complex than she already had. And if there was one thing he didn't want on his conscience, it was hurting another woman.

Gemma was covered up in an extra-large t-shirt. She was flicking through a glossy magazine, but he could see that she was anything but casual. Snagging his boxer briefs from the bed, he made himself decent, before getting back on the bed.

Her eyes flicked toward him, expectation apparent.

"I'm nothing more than something bad that happened to a woman people loved."

It was not enough of an explanation, that half-thought-out sentence. But it was the easiest thing he could think of without revealing who he really was and having her asking him to go. Because he wanted to stay.

Her mouth opened. Closed. Then she started to speak.

"What—"

The dog barked. Gemma's eyes snapped to the closed door. The sound of the dog dropping something then running toward the front door filled the quiet house.

In a flash, Gemma jammed her feet into a short pair of those shearling boots every woman in Los Angeles seemed to own.

"Who is it?" he asked before he realized he didn't have the right to know the answer to his question.

"I have no idea," she said, walking over and throwing open the door.

It only took a few seconds for him to realize that no man should leave a woman unprotected, especially someone as vulnerable as Gemma. As quickly as he could, he shoved his legs into his jeans and ran after her.

He was too late. Sylvester Poole caught sight of him. The manager's eyes pinged between Gemma, then Adonis, then back again. A sense of knowing lifted his chin.

"This is cozy."

Gemma colored, her pale skin turning a deep, deep red.

"We were just...discussing the remaining work that needs to be done downstairs," she mumbled.

Sylvester's eyes scanned the room. There was nothing Adonis could do to hide their half-clothed state. But the lack of plans spread on the table, the lack of planning notebook, and the fact that there wasn't a single light or lantern made her words a lie. A polite lie that a decent person would leave alone. Sylvester wasn't striking Adonis as a decent person. If anyone could tell good from bad, it was him.

Sylvester didn't prove him wrong. He continued, "On a Saturday night. On your birthday. It may be your birthday, hon, but *I* wasn't born yesterday. Okay?"

"Did you need something, Sylvester?" Gemma asked, recovering her composure in a seriously quick amount of time. Had to be her acting training. It took him days to recover from the smallest slight.

"You didn't answer your phone this morning. You know I can't let that go unchecked."

Gemma nodded thoughtfully. He decided to let the two talk about whatever business they needed to discuss and maybe retrieve his shirt from the bedroom.

In that instant, Granger dropped his bone with a thud and came to Adonis, sitting and leaning hard against his leg. He tried to shift his foot and the dog leaned harder, thwarting his escape plan.

"Maybe we'll have to establish a new protocol."

"Anyway, here's your gift from your agent." He thrust a slim envelope into her ready hands. "When I told him I was coming, he asked me to drop it off. Oh, and I have something from Elton Lamb."

Her sigh was world weary. Adonis was starting to think that for all she had, she wasn't getting much of what she needed.

"What did he send? Did you tell him that I'm not doing another movie with him?"

"Did you read the script he sent? It's really good. Golden Globe, if not Oscar worthy."

"Are you dangling awards in front of me, Sylvester? Do I need to remind you, I have a box full of them?"

"From when you were a kid, Gemma. You need to prove yourself as an adult actress. Jodie Foster did it and look at her now. No one's talking about *Taxi Driver* anymore."

"No offense, but I'm done with being the victim. I can't do something like *The Accused*."

Adonis patted the dog. Granger stood in anticipation. "Excuse me," he said. He quickly strode toward the stairs, taking this opportunity to spare Gemma further embarrassment.

When he was dressed and as put together as a man could be after mind-blowing sex, he followed the voices to the driveway.

He stepped out to find Sylvester and Gemma standing in front of a car whose doors opened like wings.

"What is that?" Adonis asked.

"Elton's gift. Some kind of plug-in car. Somehow, I can save the world from global warming in this. No mention of the huge amount of raw materials and resources necessary to produce said car."

"He really wanted you to have this," Sylvester said.

"How'd you get it here?"

"I drove it."

"Take it back."

"He'll be pissed."

"What is he going to do, blacklist me? It's not the McCarthy era. You keep it. Where's the log book?"

"What is that?"

"The papers that show who's the owner of the car."

Sylvester messed around in the glove box. "Can't find it right now. I had it this morning…"

"When you find it, messenger it to me. I'll sign it over to you or whomever you need to impress."

"Ah, Gemma, you're putting me in an awkward position."

"Fine, Sylvester. Fine. Thanks for the birthday wishes, because somewhere in all this I'm sure you wished me a happy birthday. Now I'm going to call Elton at home on a Saturday night. You have a good night." Turning on her heel, Gemma walked into her house. After she swept the dog's tail from harm, she slammed the door.

"Feisty like a redhead, huh?" Sylvester looked at him under hooded lids.

Adonis employed all the skills he'd learned in recovery and didn't take the bait.

"Good seeing you. I'll…uh…send you a progress report this weekend. Think we're ahead of schedule. Definitely will get this all done by Thanksgiving like I promised."

Sylvester clicked a button. The rear doors closed with a slow, graceful arc.

"Gonna take this home and put it in the drive. Never know if she'll change her mind."

"Looked like she made a decision to me," Adonis said. He'd been on the receiving end of a final decision. He didn't think Gemma was one to change her mind often.

"Yeah, well. I've known her for going on fifteen years."

"Gotta get going myself," he said. As much as

Sylvester made his skin crawl, he was glad for the interruption. For a moment back there, he'd let his guard down. He'd been about to lay all his crap out there for Gemma to see. Sex and intimacy weren't the same thing. He was glad he'd realized that.

He jingled his keys meaningfully. "You're blocking the exit."

"Oh, right. No problem, bro, I'll get out of your way. Gotta get going, huh? I know how awful those morning-afters can be. Gotta get out before you're driving down to Carbon Beach for breakfast."

As they stood outside in the now-crowded driveway, Sylvester looked left and right as if the live oak and magnolia trees flanking the property had ears. "Was she anything like her sex tape?"

Adonis kept his fisted hand at his side. If he'd learned a single lesson in his life, it was that impulsive actions rarely, if ever, had good results.

Instead he said again, "Good seeing you," nodded, got in his van, and wondered all the way home what in the hell her manager had been talking about.

Sex tape?

How could someone who'd never had sex have a tape?

ELEVEN

Adonis

A sex tape.

A virgin.

A liar.

The same three thoughts chased him north on the Ventura Freeway. All the way from Malibu to Oxnard. The two places were as polar opposites as a sex tape and a virgin. On the PCH, on the 101, he went over it all again and again. Gemma, both bashful and ballsy in equal measure, asking for sex. Then admitting she was inexperienced.

Framing a house without plans was easier to put together than this puzzle.

The minute he stepped through his hollow-core apartment door, he headed for the fridge. Ten minutes later, he sat down at the two-person table in the kitchen, turkey sandwich in one hand, canned Arnold Palmer in the other.

The dusty laptop he took to projects, that he'd left on the kitchen table charging, glowed like a beacon.

If there was one place to look for a sex tape, it would be the Internet. He wolfed down the sandwich and stood up. He was a little less hungry and a whole lot more restless.

Why would she lie? He didn't really know her well enough to answer that question. Maybe she thought she'd had to do the virgin routine to get him interested. He'd be lying if he said that hadn't fueled his attraction. Hadn't that been the thing that had pushed him from more than casual interest and over the edge into willingness?

Something primal in him was drawn to being her first. The first to…

Or not.

He wasn't the first. He'd gotten snowed by a Hollywood star—an expert at snow jobs.

Shoving the dusty laptop under the arm of the shirt that had been pristine hours ago, he jogged from his apartment to his van. The engine was still warm when he shoved the laptop under the passenger seat. He knew where to get the kick in the pants he needed.

He'd stopped seeking out his father's advice and approval years ago. The health scare from earlier this year had made him want his father more. He didn't need Dominic, but wanted to get some of that wisdom before his father was gone.

"Again?" his father said an hour later. "I see you maybe twice a year, and now you've essentially moved to Los Angeles County. Come on in. It's practically a party in here."

He'd been so far in his own head, that he hadn't realized his father's house was anything other than quiet.

If he'd been paying attention, he'd have driven right on by.

Right on by when he saw the driveway stacked with cars. Right on by when he saw the house lights blazing. Crowds were not his thing. The church basement meetings he'd attended for the last many years were about all he could take of community.

The smell of garlic assaulted him first. Oregano was next. Then he saw the meze table—the traditional setup of Greek appetizers. Around that table sat all of his immediate family.

Awkward turned into uncomfortable. Talking and laughing ceased. Zoe and Nicki looked up at him. Holly played polite, smiles hovering around her lips.

"It's the black sheep coming to visit. I'll try not to eat your young. Carry on."

His lame attempt at tackling the elephant in the living room fell flat. As flat as the last deflated pita remaining in the center of the table.

Defeat and sadness descended on him like a wet blanket. One hundred eighty degrees from how he'd been feeling hours ago, when he'd been on top of the world. If not on top, at least not carrying the weight of it on his shoulders.

"I told you we should have called him," Holly whispered. In the silence of the room, that whisper was nearly a shout.

"Traffic is a bear from Ventura County." With that, he tried to excuse them. But the bottom line was that he hadn't been invited. They'd thought of him, and passed him over. When he'd turned down ninety-nine percent of invitations for drinks, dinner, and parties, they'd eventually stopped. But not being invited was like a kick in the gut. Unlike the puzzle of Gemma Hart, this one was easy to assemble. He'd been Donny Downer one too many gatherings.

"Have a seat," Dominic said. "I'll go to the kitchen and scare you up something to drink."

Everyone shifted in their seats again. He looked around. Zoe, Nicki, and Holly all had something alcoholic in hand. It was always the same at parties or any social gathering. And even if it no longer made him uncomfortable, it still brought a halt to everyone else's fun. So he stood awkwardly waiting for his dad.

"Berry lemonade or limeade?" Dominic asked as he came back into the living/dining room area. He held two different bottles of fizzy drinks in his hands.

"Limeade," he said.

"Have a seat," Nicki repeated, moving a bit on the couch.

Maybe it had been awkward because Adonis had been standing at the door like a specter. He crowded in between Nicki and his wife, setting the laptop awkwardly near his feet.

"Who that?" Iris said, wiggling on her father's lap and pointing to Adonis.

"That's your uncle Adonis," Holly said, standing and picking up her baby. "Do you want to hold her?"

"She can walk, right?" Didn't people stop holding babies once they walked? Or maybe his mom had because she'd had two, then three, and couldn't hold them all.

"You should hold her." Not taking a hint from his

crossed arms, Holly delivered the child to him like a parcel.

His eyes roamed the room wildly, looking for someone to save him from this onslaught of child. Not a single person met his eyes, save for Zoe, who looked like she was barely able to contain her laughter at his discomfort.

"Hello, little Iris," he said. "I'm Adonis. I'm Nicki's older brother."

The girl looked at him as if he were an alien. Her eyes roamed his face and clothes. Then pronouncing him acceptable, Iris laid her head on his chest.

In a way he'd never anticipated, the toddler relaxed him. With this child on his lap, it was like he disappeared, stopped being the center of attention. Made him wonder if that's what Granger did for Gemma.

Gemma.

The sex tape.

It all came hurtling back, the reason he'd driven down here. He'd wanted his father to talk him out of looking her up. Because if there was anyone with a bit of life wisdom to dole out, it was Dominic.

"What's up with the mysterious, elusive Gemma Hart?" Nicki asked. The poke in the ribs his fiancée gave him was subtle, but Adonis still saw it. His sister, as always, refused to make further eye contact.

Had he known she was in the house, he'd have turned his van around and gone home the way he came. Though he wanted to resolve the friction between them and close the chasm that yawned, it was easier to avoid all of it. Kick the can far down the road, to the next century maybe.

After her last few months in town, he was starting to believe that some fractures could never be healed.

"Have you ever seen her?" Nick asked. "Dad said he shook her hand only once before he came to with her standing over him, phone in hand, making excuses as to why she couldn't dial nine-one-one."

Do not blush. Do not get red in the face. Self-talk might work for swearing off alcohol, but not for the blood that surged from his heart outward.

"Hot," Iris said, lifting her head from his chest.

"Babies are like little furnaces," he said. It was the best excuse he could muster in five seconds.

"Let me take her," Holly said. The little bundle of person disappeared, and instead of more grounded, he felt more vulnerable.

"Adonis went on a date with her," Dominic boasted from his position by the kitchen door. Seconds later, he came in with saganaki still sizzling in a tiny pan. He slid the fried cheese onto an empty wooden board next to crushed lemon and sliced bread.

That appetizer, which usually earned oohs and aahs from a crowd, did nothing tonight. The open mouths weren't agape with hunger, but with shock. Dates with A-list celebrities probably didn't happen too often in any crowd.

"We went for a walk on the beach," he said into the expectant silence.

"That's it? A walk on the beach?" Nicki poked. Little brothers. He wanted to shove this one, with his probing questions, far from him. He didn't think Dominic would appreciate a wrestling match between grown men in his living room.

"I took her flowers for her birthday tonight," he said, to satisfy their curiosity.

Pan and potholder long gone, Dominic came back into the living room, ouzo in one hand, spring water in the other. He topped off the glasses of those who looked like they were ready for more. His father placed the bottles on the built-in and stood by the studded club chair where Zoe sat unmoving.

"What in heaven's name are you doing here then?" Dominic deliberately looked at the clock decorating the mantel.

"I, um, gave her the flowers. Her manager came by. They needed to talk…"

"That Sylvester guy is nice enough. Kind of makes me a little bit…I don't know…something."

"He's not a gentleman," Adonis found himself blurting out. "When I was getting in my van, he asked if I'd seen her sex tape."

As if his unexpected presence hadn't been enough, he'd gone and said that. It was like tossing a hand grenade into a room. But that had always been his issue. He fucked up social situations, first with the binge drinking, now with the world's most inappropriate topics.

Holly's eyes bulged.

Gesturing toward sleepy-eyed Iris, he said, "Oh, sorry. Kid and all that."

"I'm sure she won't be scarred for life," Nicki said.

Holly didn't look so sure. His soon-to-be sister-in-law

stood and took Iris from the room. Five minutes later, she came back childless.

"Set her down in the Pack 'n Play, Dominic. She was tired."

"Of course. I'll go check in on her in a minute. Sit, put your feet up. I hear the ottoman's comfortable." Everyone laughed. Adonis didn't get the joke.

"Sex tape?" Holly asked, once she was comfortable. "Like Kim Kardashian?"

"I don't know. Seems like the kind of thing I shouldn't really get into. It's private, right?" he asked in a backhanded search for advice.

"You had your computer under your arm when you got here. Were you going to have Dad look up Gemma's tape for you?" Nicki asked through his laughter.

Adonis didn't let on that his brother wasn't too far from the truth.

"Gemma Hart has one?" Zoe asked, speaking for the first time.

"Are you kidding me? It was the scandal of the year maybe five years ago, maybe more. You know the angle, child star all grown up," Nicki said.

Zoe's eyes zoomed to his, ready to condemn. "Did you watch it?"

"Invasion of privacy isn't my cup of tea," he said. What happened between two or more consenting adults was very much private in his mind.

All eyes turned on Dominic when he let out a disbelieving snort.

"Don't look at me. I've never seen it. I prefer my ladies older. But if you're interested in having a relationship, it's with her. Not her past, not her job. With *her*. I'd pretend you never heard a thing from Sylvester."

Adonis might have been an asshole one too many times in his life, but he wasn't going to tell his whole family about that virgin claim because it was either the most private thing one lover could share with another, or it would make him look like the fool he was starting to think he was.

"What's this about you liking your ladies older, Dad? Are you seeing someone?" Deflection was a tool he'd honed to sharpness.

All attention turned to Dominic, when their always self-assured, very wise father started to stutter.

"I should get some more napkins. Those linen ones aren't doing the job. I think I have some paper—"

"Not so fast," Zoe was saying to their father's retreating back. "Not so fast."

Dominic halted then turned. He walked back into the room, confidence in his stride.

"I guess I should tell you all first, the people I love most in the world. I'm going to start dating again. I've watched all of you pair up, and now it's my turn," he said.

"Oh, is it with the Bridget woman?" Zoe asked. "She was so cute when she was helping out. She's your friend's mother, right?" she asked, turning to Holly for confirmation.

"Her boyfriend's mother, actually," Holly answered.

"It's not Bridget," Dominic insisted. "I'm just thinking I'm not ready to spend the rest of my life alone. I've got some years left."

"Wait. So what happened? I thought you and Bridget had gone out a few times," Zoe said.

"Funny, you weren't a fan of my dating a few months ago."

"I wanted you to get well first," his sister sputtered.

Dominic's raised eyebrow told everyone he didn't believe any of the shit Zoe was shoveling. "Look, dear heart, it didn't work out. She mainly wanted a handyman. Now that her house is almost done, she realized I wasn't that interesting."

"Ouch. Sorry," Zoe said, looking suitably chastised. "I hear that the percentages are in your favor though. It's gotta be something like sixty percent women in your age bracket."

Adonis felt bad that it hadn't worked out with that woman his dad had met. But with the old-world charm Dominic oozed, he wasn't worried that his dad would spend any time alone.

The room was quiet for a long moment. He picked up a plate and took a little of all the dishes. He started with an olive. The salty, savory tartness was a shock to his tongue. It reminded him of having this same spread so many times. Of his father and Uncle Alessandro sitting around various living rooms, drinking, smoking cigars, and eating. Always eating.

Would the dishes have been Italian if his mother had lived longer? Lasagna instead of pastitsio, meatballs with marinara instead of tzatziki.

Once the talking started back up, he rose and went into the butler's pantry.

He paused under the arched entrance. His sister was

already there, standing with sketchpad in hand. It was like a throwback to their childhood. How many times had he walked in on her in one room or another, to find her deep in concentration, pouring her energy into one drawing or another?

"Sorry," he said.

Zoe's head snapped up while her hand paused in mid-pencil stroke. His sister jammed the pencil behind her ear. "I can leave."

"Don't leave, Zoe."

Three feet yawned between them, the gap as wide as Copper Canyon.

"What do we have to say to each other?"

"By my count, a lot. Quite a lot."

Eyebrows raised, Zoe tapped her boot-clad foot with expectation.

"I want what we used to have."

"What's that?"

"A close brother-sister relationship. For most of my life, Zoe, you were my best friend. It's like I lost you *and* Emily that night, only you didn't die. You lived. I lived."

"But—"

"Nothing. Not one single sacrifice, or deal with God above in heaven, will bring Emily Little back to life. I know that more deeply and profoundly than you could imagine."

"It's like you got away with murder. It's never seemed fair."

"I'm tired of being the bad penny. I'm tired of every interaction with this family being so awful. It's like hurricane Adonis came through and you all talk about what happened in my wake. It was devastating. We have to pick up the pieces though and move on. How many years is enough, Zoe?"

Impatiently, his sister brushed away tears. His tall, stoic sister, whom he'd always loved more than he'd loved anyone else in the world, turned and walked away.

TWELVE

Gemma

What was it about being a celebrity that made people think you were deaf? Her outdoor security system might not have bass-heavy, theater-style surround sound, but she'd heard Sylvester loud and clear. That stupid tape would follow her to the ends of the earth.

Now, in addition to wondering if Adonis had found her bedroom performance sufficient, she had to wonder if he were scouring the Internet looking for her single most humiliating performance.

Once a single copy of something existed on the Internet, it could be copied thousands if not millions of times in seconds, minutes. She'd learned that simple mathematical formula the hard way.

Her lawyers had scoured the vast reaches of the globe, shooting out warning letters like bullets to website owners who willfully violated her privacy. Which had worked — in the United States and Western Europe. But China and Russia were like the Wild West of the Internet.

No amount of threats or lawsuits shut down those sites anchored in foreign countries. If their governments applied any pressure at all, and that was a big if, the sites shut down, and in the next breath, a new one popped up in their places.

After a few years, she got tired of paying four hundred dollars per hour to have someone with a law degree play the legal equivalent of the arcade game Whack-A-Mole. So the sex tape's digital tracks lingered, easy enough to find by anyone with patience.

Gemma Hart duped by one Andrew O'Bryan.

It had to be why Adonis had left after one of the most significant days of her life. The presence of a sex tape made everything she'd said before a lie.

If he'd listen, she had so many explanations, a handful, a bundle. Gemma would happily heap them all on his lap for him to sort through, believe.

If he'd stayed.

But he'd left.

Run away like she was made of some kind of radioactive material. But maybe she was. Giovanni kept saying she had to let people in. Every person she did let through her defenses disappointed her in some way, big or small. Her hope that Adonis would somehow be different, especially if she were in charge, wasn't at all turning out like she'd expected. He'd disappointed her from his first refusal. Then after she'd turned his no into a yes, he'd left anyway.

The buzzer sounded on time, and Gemma pressed the button, releasing the gate. The familiar yellow van eased up the twisting rise, disappearing then reappearing.

Adonis parked where he always did, off to the side so as not to block her access.

Gemma girded all that needed girding, and stepped out the front door. Words of explanation died on her lips when Dominic's truck immediately followed up the drive. The older Andreis hopped out of his truck before the younger. So much for a long talk.

"Time got freed up, Ms. Hart. Two for the price of one today. How's that? We'll get everything ready for the cabinet installers to come tomorrow. We'll all be outta your red hair in no time."

Dominic was already pulling tools and machines out of the back of the van, when Adonis opened his own door. The jolt that zinged from her belly to her toes was unexpected. Or maybe she should have expected it. From the day he'd taken over for his dad, he'd made her feel something where she'd been feeling a lot of nothing for a long time.

"Um, hi," she gibbered out. She wanted to grab him by the shoulders, pull him down for a kiss. But she'd been raised on the wrong side of Europe. Public displays of affection were for those on the continent. She was stiff upper lips and all that.

"Good morning. We'll be making a bit of noise today, but with Dad here, we can have the cabinet guys come tomorrow." She looked at his eyes, shifted her gaze to his throat, his hands. She could see nothing of the affection that he'd heaped on her a mere two days before.

"I thought they weren't due for a couple of weeks." She was trying to remember what Adonis had said about the schedule, but she'd been looking at his strong arms and thinking about beds, not calendars.

"Your stuff is done early," Adonis said, as if getting out of her house quickly was the most important thing in the world. "It's easier for the carpenters if they can use their studio space for making new cabinets instead of storage for yours. Most clients are happy to have a project come in early."

"I'd hoped…" She didn't finish. The words "practice" and "repeat performance" bounced around her brain, but neither was appropriate with a parent around.

"You'd hoped what?" he asked like a builder instead of a lover.

"Right. You get to it. I'll make myself scarce." As fast as she could without running, or looking like the scared hares that ran from her parents' dogs, she was out of the room.

At least she hadn't shown up to the door stark naked. Twice, she'd thought better of that. Both times, she was supremely happy that she had. Imagine the heart attack she'd have given Dominic.

The knock on her bedroom door nearly sent her through the beamed ceiling. Asking who it was passed through her mind. But who asked "who is it?" through a door inside their own home?

After dropping the latest glossy edition of *Tatler* magazine that was hardly keeping her attention, Gemma walked to the door and pulled it open with a swift jerk.

She simultaneously wanted to pummel him and hug him. He made the choice for her and did that one thing that disarmed her every time. He fisted a hand in her hair

—this time in a messy bun she'd twisted in frustration—and tilted her head, making her ready to receive his kiss.

And she wanted that kiss. More than recriminations. More than explanations. The magic of that connection they'd had had haunted her all weekend. It was still there like a weak nuclear force.

She stopped his hand when it tugged at the J-shaped zipper pull on her sweatshirt.

"Your dad?" she asked. Despite her worldwide reputation for it, she was not interested in public displays.

"Went out to search for a double-gang box extender," he explained.

It did not compute for her. "Double-gang—"

"Means he'll be gone at least an hour. Maybe two if the taco truck he likes is out there. He likes tongue."

Tacos and body parts made her head spin. Or it was him, standing there all strong muscles and clean sweat, the faintest hint of sawdust on his cheeks.

Before she could think better of it, she lifted her hand, cupped his jaw, and brushed at the tiny tan specs of curling wood.

"It's not smart. It's not rational. But I want you, Gemma. Now. Here."

It was daft, and not all that thought out, but she wanted him too. Instead of admitting her growing weakness for him the way he'd just done, she guided him down until his lips met hers again. Holding nothing back, she plundered his mouth as he did the same.

All of her modesty, and hesitation, and shyness disappeared in the face of now. In the face of what she knew he could make her feel. The urge, suddenly, to be free of her velour tracksuit was undeniable.

Stepping back, she made quick work of removing her clothes. A heap of velour and silk was all that was left when she turned to walk toward the bed.

"Not so fast," he said. Adonis snagged her hand and led her to the orange chair by the door. She'd never sat in the leather seat her interior designer had said was an accent piece, a counterpoint in design, or something like that. Something for show, not for sitting.

"Why?" Fast is what she wanted. Fast is what they needed.

"Wait."

Without removing a stitch of his own clothing, Adonis knelt before her, and all of it — the inexperience, the nervousness — came rushing back.

"I'm sorry…"

"Don't be sorry for your desires, Gemma. You deserve pleasure just as much as the next person, no matter what your resume."

"Oh…" Her next words were lost, swallowed, forgotten when his head descended, when his strong, work-roughened hands braced against the insides of her knees, thighs. When he hooked under her legs and pulled her forward and feasted upon her as if he were a starving man and she was a banquet.

"You taste like the sun, moon, and stars," he whispered, the words vibrating against her most sensitive flesh.

He might have said something more. He must have said something more because she'd followed some urgent command to hold on to the arms of the chair like she were holding on for dear life. Then it was all twisty and tight below her belly. She sucked in her breath, holding on to the pleasure until that very last minute when she couldn't hold on anymore and all she wanted to do was let go, let the waves of feeling pulse along her body, making her all lightheaded and giddy and ready to tie him to her bed so he could do this again and again, and never leave.

All at once, he was shoving down his pants, fitting on a condom, and lifting her. To keep upright, she wound her arms tight about his neck and shoulders. The smell of her and him mingled with the heady scent of sex.

He shifted his hands and before she could gather breath, he'd impaled her. In just two days, she'd forgotten that he could make her feel so full, so wanted. Adonis' eyes never left her. They roamed appreciatively over her face, hair, breasts, and all the rest. Appraisal that would normally have her squirming in her skin did exactly the opposite. It made her feel like everyone else for once. Human.

Nothing more.

Nothing less.

If her arms weren't turning into jelly, she could have stayed like that for hours. Adonis pumping into her oh so slowly, panting out his appreciation and desire. Her answering hiccough of arousal as a second wave came over her. But it didn't last forever, no matter how hard she tried to hold on to the sensation. His rhythm eventually broke, turning into rapid thrusts that stoked her banked fire, until both were raging. Until she came squeezing him, milking an orgasm from him.

Carefully, as if she were the Queen's china, he lifted her and set her back upon the orange leather accent chair.

A chair she'd certainly never be able to look at without reliving just this moment.

Awkwardly, and without a word, he shuffled to the bathroom.

A quick glance at the clock told her an hour had long passed. They were in discovery danger. So she scooped up her clothes and put them all back into place, zipping her jacket to the throat, hiding the tender flesh she was sure, even without looking in the mirror, was well abraded by his soft, spiky stubble.

Needing something to come down, she wandered to the dresser and poured herself a glass of sherry. Turning a second glass over, she poured a small amount for Adonis.

The pocket door lumbered open.

"I borrowed an extra toothbrush," he said.

She tried not to squirm with all that phrase implied. Her mind reached out, grasping for purchase.

"Why'd you leave on Saturday?" It wasn't at all what she'd meant to ask. Why *wouldn't* he leave? She'd made it clear, in no uncertain terms, that she needed him for a service. Once rendered, he'd felt free to go. Now that he'd come back without her begging or cajoling, the question had frothed to the top of her mind and bubbled from her mouth.

"I needed to figure out if you'd lied to me."

She wanted to play dumb, act like an actress with no brain between her ears. She'd done it dozens of times to get what she wanted, avoid what she didn't.

Not now. Somehow, this seemed like the time to tell the truth. But the lump in her throat wouldn't cooperate.

Her mouth wouldn't let her form the right words. And the right words were so very necessary at this point.

The buzzer sounded, as if on cue.

"I have to go let your dad back in," she said without hesitation. It was so much easier talking about doors, gates and codes, than talking about Andrew O'Bryan.

"Answer me, Gemma."

"Later. When your dad is safely tucked in bed. I promise to tell you exactly what you need to know."

Later came after sundown. Later, after she'd walked Granger, inspected the handiwork of father and son Andreis, her gate buzzed. Elation and dread were with her in equal measure.

He was silent upon reentry.

The moment the door closed and the electronic lock clicked, she said, "I didn't have sex with Andrew O'Bryan."

"Who's that?"

"Andy O'Bryan, rehab rebound extraordinaire." When no sign of recognition crossed Adonis' face, she continued. "He's an actor. Really talented. Brilliant really. Has a massive cocaine addiction. Despite all that, he works, all the time. When he's not here in Malibu or Rancho Mirage at one recovery program or another, he's on set."

She could practically see the light bulb of recognition go on above Adonis' head. It was the same light bulb that winked on when someone stared at her a beat too long as they put it together in their head that she was, in the flesh, the same woman they'd seen on the big screen.

"Let's go upstairs. The second bedroom... Just come," she said. Her liquor cabinet was temporarily relocated in that room. She'd need a drink or twenty to talk about this. Plus her big computer was up there. It was both a show and tell kind of thing.

"He's been in like dozens of movies," he said after he'd taken a seat on the small couch she'd jammed into the room, along with the bed that had already been there and the table she was using as a temporary desk and drink-mixing corner.

"Yes, loads."

"He's sober though, right? Has been for a decade. I'm sure I saw that on some TV interview."

For the briefest moment, she thought it odd that Adonis would know anything about Andy, but maybe he was as much a tabloid checkout-stand reader as most Americans were. It was one trend that she wished the UK had kept all nice and tidy on her side of the pond, with its strong libel and privacy laws keeping it all in check. The American celebrity free-for-all was horrid for everyone in her business.

"Don't know. Wouldn't bet my life on that," she said. She knew better than anyone that what was written so very rarely reflected the truth.

"So, O'Bryan..."

"Watch," she said in answer. She pressed the spacebar on the little keyboard and all fifteen minutes of ignominious glory lit up the screen.

She wanted to get down on her knees and thank Giovanni for her ability to stand in this room at this moment not wanting to die of shame.

Instead of watching the video, because she'd been there, she watched Adonis. And if experiencing it hadn't burned the searing memory in her brain, being bombarded by clips of it over and over again surely did.

The video started with O'Bryan in the bedroom of his Bel Air mansion. She hated the word mansion in the States, but all twenty thousand square feet of O'Bryan's house couldn't be described in any other manner. In the video, the dark-walled and coffered-ceilinged room was flooded with light from the open windows and California sun. He adjusted the camera position. Coke-fueled rapid-fire speech blasted from the speakers hidden in corners of the room.

"Folks, you're about to see the great deflowering of Hollywood's sweetheart, Gemma Hart. If you've turned on your television for more than a moment, then you know that we've been seeing each other since the filming of *Entwined Souls*.

"As things have heated up between us, she's shared a secret with me that she's never told anyone else. Gemma Hart is a virgin." O'Bryan did a mock double-take.

"I know, right? But that aunt Sharon of hers has kept a tight leash on her all these years. At least that's what Gemma says. From what I've seen of Sharon Hart though, Gemma's inherited some wild woman genes. Coming right up, we'll get to see. Is she a Madonna or a whore in bed? I'd lay Vegas odds on the first one, but you never know. Maybe the British have some secret steam. Stay tuned." O'Bryan stroked his own jaw in obvious self-admiration. "Damn, I should have gone out for the part of that TV news anchor in *Earthquake: Aftershock*. I'm pretty damned good at these teasers."

At least Adonis wasn't laughing at O'Bryan's crude

attempt at humor. O'Bryan had, of course, been the star of the huge blockbuster *Earthquake* and its sequel. Her agent had gleefully informed her, in his usual tone-deaf manner, that O'Bryan had been paid forty million for the first, sixty for the second.

The video jump cut. The room was a bit darker with the plantation shutters closed. O'Bryan winked at the camera before she walked into the room. No matter how evolved she became or how much she'd talked this out with Giovanni, Gemma had to turn her head.

Adonis' swift intake of breath told her he wasn't blind, and unlike her, hadn't tuned out. Into the movie frame she'd walked, all Fredrick's of Hollywood. Dolled up like a professional. How she'd spent hours trying to get sexy just right, and failing miserably. She looked like a tarted-up teenager trying to sneak into a central London club. It wasn't much of a good look on anyone at fifteen, and it wasn't a good look on Gemma in her twenties.

O'Bryan had his profile facing the camera. Most directors she'd known wouldn't use that angle to open a scene. When O'Bryan's pants dropped and he lifted his erect penis from his briefs, the reason for the positioning became obvious.

"I can't watch this," Adonis said, hitting a key that stopped the action.

"I've seen it hundreds of times," she said after a fortifying sip of sherry. "It gets easier."

"Can't you tell me what happens?"

"I'll fast forward."

Mouse in hand, she scrolled to the half eleven mark. Just after the knob-polishing bit, the screen appeared to go to static. When the fuzz cleared away, Gemma was lying on the extra-large king-size, topless. Her bottom, at least, was covered by Andy's duvet.

"Are you sleeping?" Adonis asked, his expression puzzled.

"Since I wasn't on a coke bender, I got tired." She left out the copious amounts of alcohol O'Bryan had plied her with. Not that she was blaming him. She'd been as keen to drink that night as he'd been to get her pissed. She hadn't had the coke to offset the effects of alcohol like he'd had though.

O'Bryan's face filled the camera's frame. "I swear," he said. "The batteries on this Flip are the worst. They're supposed to last two hours, man. But I had to set it up early. So…you missed it folks. But let me tell you, it was good. She was so ripe, so sweet. A little bit of a whore, way more Madonna. But I'm sure I can change that. Virgins are my favorite flavor."

She watched Adonis watch O'Bryan walk over to her. The coked-up actor tweaked her nipples, jiggled her breasts for the camera, then followed with more lewd pantomiming.

"There's no sex on the sex tape?" Adonis asked, turning from the computer.

"Can we not debate the definition of sex like a certain American president? It was all very much *Brown Bunny* for a good ten minutes."

"*Brown Bunny*? Is that some kind of English phrase?"

"No. It's a crap movie where the writer slash director slash star ends his film with a ten-minute oral sex sequence where he's the recipient."

"Seriously?"

"American cinema. What can I say?"

"So…"

"So O'Bryan walked about telling everyone in the world he shagged me. Anyone's best guess is that he sold the tape to a Russian media network. Don't know how much money he got."

"He sold you out for cash?"

"I don't really care about that part. But he was on every teatime entertainment chat show. I got lewd suggestions over meetings with directors, he got an eighty-million-dollar payday the next year. But to answer your other question, I didn't lie to you. We never had inter-course. I may not be that smart, but I knew better than to do it with him."

"Did you want to?"

"I thought I did. I thought I would. But he was high. I have no idea if he loved me like he said. I'm not even sure he liked me. Doesn't matter. I made my choice that night. And believe it or not, in that, he honored my decision. He violated me in a thousand ways, a million different times, but not that night."

"Did he go into recovery after that?"

"Yes. No. Maybe." She shook her head in dismissal. "Does it matter? Addiction is no excuse for bad behavior."

"Amends?"

"Now it's *you* speaking the foreign language. What do you mean?" She squinted, trying to make heads or tails of his question.

"Did he make amends? You know, apologize, I guess. Try to fix this."

"I'm sorry I shot your dog." Gemma threw up her hands in exasperation.

"What?"

"It's like the neighbor coming to your cottage saying he shot your best hunting dog by accident. Sure, Andy came to apologize. I was at the agency for a meeting. He was there, I think, signing the papers making him the highest-paid actor in history."

"What did he say?"

"I'm in a tiny room with my agent, Sylvester, and some kind of intern. Andy comes in with his super-agent, and an entire entourage who probably got a conference room the size of an ocean liner. I haven't been in that room, with its one-hundred-eighty-degree view of Hollywood, in ten years." God, she'd shown her petty self-pitying side. Course correction was in order. She continued the story, minus the pity. "My agent stops my meeting so he can speak. 'Sorry for the tape,' O'Bryan says. 'Now that I'm sober, I see that I've hurt you. I'm here to make amends.' That's the word you said, right?"

Adonis nodded in confirmation. Then he frowned. "That's it?"

"I had no effing clue what he was talking about. He's done about a thousand shitty things, and he'd never apologized for the tape. So Sylvester asks what he's going to do. Andy's assistant tosses a check on the table. 'Maybe you can donate to Monica Lewinsky's foundation or something.'"

"How much?"

"Ten million." Gemma shrugged. No amount of money could wipe away what he'd done.

"What did you do?"

"Made an anonymous donation."

"Does Monica Lewinsky have a foundation?"

"I have no idea," she said. For a long couple of days, she'd read everything she could get her hands on about the White House intern. In the end, she thought Monica had been lucky that the only evidence of her stupidity had been a blue dress. Life before the Internet had been grand. "I gave it away to the RSPCA."

"Is that a group for exploited women?"

"I hardly think a couple of other clueless actresses and I count in the realm of exploited women. I made a bad choice. I can't say about the others. It's possible they did it for the exposure. Can't truly know. It's the Royal Society for the Prevention of Cruelty to Animals." It was and always had been the most worthy cause in her eyes, protecting those who could not protect themselves.

"Have you forgiven him?"

"Forgiven Andrew O'Bryan for ruining my life? Making me the laughing stock of the industry? For having stupid clips of this video, with tiny plaster-size censor strips across my chest, showing up next to anything I've ever done? No, I'd say that I haven't yet found the power to forgive the little entitled shit."

"Entitled?"

"His father is Elton Lamb."

Adonis didn't pretend not to know Lamb. Even unplugged Montana survivalists had heard of the world-famous director. "Didn't know that."

"One of Hollywood's dirty little secrets. Half the

people I work with are related to each other. Nothing like being discovered in your backyard sandbox."

"Sorry."

"Nothing to be sorry about. I fell into this, and here I stay. Part of me wants out. But you know what? I don't have any other marketable skills, except dog training."

"I'm sorry I questioned you about the tape. It was inappropriate."

"Oh, yeah, okay," she said, taken aback by his imme-diate apology.

"I should have taken your word for it on something that was so important to you."

"You sound positively enlightened. That's a relief." Most men would have stammered around their stupid statements, never fully apologizing for their crap assumptions.

His smile, so rare, lit up the room. It made her want to celebrate. "You must have some sherry. I'd offer cham-pagne, but until the wine fridge is installed, everything's in storage down on the west side. There's a place near the Four-oh-five freeway, if you can believe it, that stores wine —"

"I can't."

"Of course you can. Let me get you a glass. It's nothing expensive, by any means. I want to toast to us being on the same page. You don't think I'm a lying slag and I know you're not a caveman."

She fished around for a clean glass. She'd put the earlier one in a bin to be washed later. But she was sure there were a couple of clean ones left. The service that came to take the dishes wasn't due until day after tomorrow.

"You should forgive O'Bryan. People do all sorts of crappy things. Have you considered that it was the addiction, not him?"

"I think I'm going to take back everything I said about you not being a caveman. Some actor who neither lacks for work nor money sneaks pictures of me, half naked, performing, doing…" She'd gotten to a point where she could watch the video, but saying it out loud was still hard. "And you think it's his addiction?" Not his penis or vanity, she wanted to add, but didn't because talking about such things was crass.

"Sometimes it takes people hitting rock bottom before they can come out the other side a better person."

"You don't even know Andy O'Bryan. Or do you? Please don't tell me you're some big fan, here to tell me to sit down and be quiet. Because he's rich and famous, that it's okay to take advantage of me. Don't think I haven't heard it before. A thousand times, from a thousand people. Please tell me that's not what you're saying."

Her head was going to literally explode. Leaving tiny pieces of brain matter all over the newly painted walls.

"If there's one thing I can't stand about Hollywood, it's this town's ability to excuse men their bad behavior. Have sex with a thirteen-year-old girl, flee the country, win an Oscar."

"But I do know O'Bryan," Adonis insisted. He patted his chest like he and the actor were bosom buddies.

"You what? All along, you…and you didn't tell me."

Of all the emotions she'd prepared for, sympathy for her victimizer wasn't one of them.

"No, that's not what I meant. I don't know O'Bryan. Not personally. I've never met him or anyone who works with him. What I'm trying to say is that I could be O'Bryan. The reason I can't drink your sherry, the reason I think you should forgive him is because…"

"Because?" It was taking all of her strength to hold it together. To not kick him out and curse herself for more years of bad judgment. "Why?"

"Because I could be him."

"How could you be an entitled asshole who hurts women? Do you have a secret past I don't know about?" Adonis was astonishingly good looking in a ruggedly handsome, non-assuming way. She was starting to flip through the files in her brain, trying to place him on TV, in a commercial, in a movie. Surely she'd remember someone like him if he'd been kicking around Hollywood when she was a kid—but maybe not.

His nod was slow, sure.

She braced herself for what was about to come. It seemed as if she'd spent half her life bracing herself for directors who didn't like her work, for casting agents who could give her a job, for her aunt slash former manager's latest screw up. Bracing herself was well within her area of expertise. She nodded, ready.

Adonis' blink was slow. Then he spoke, his tone somber and deliberate.

"I'm an alcoholic, Gemma. And it took me taking someone's life before I realized it."

THIRTEEN

Adonis

He'd pressed the nuclear button.

It would be only moments before an explosion came.

Any moment now.

They'd long abandoned normal dating rituals. Coffee on the first date. Dinner and a movie on the second. Sex on the third and fourth. Trading secrets on the fifth. At least that was what was in the doctors' waiting room magazines he'd occasionally thumbed through on dating and mating.

Watching a sex tape and admission of manslaughter somehow weren't in the normal course.

Gemma knocked back her sherry as though she were in a parched desert and it was the only liquid available. After she swallowed, she asked the inevitable. "You killed someone?"

"Not on purpose."

He wondered just how much Gemma had had to drink that afternoon, because her walk from the desk to the bed was unsteady. She sank down on the bed as if it was a lover's embrace. Her sigh said she was unsure how to proceed. It was as if she was unsure of whether she wanted to know the details, the truth, any of it. She admired the ceiling beams a long time before she spoke.

"When was this?"

"About a dozen years now," he said, mentally counting on his fingers, realizing that it was more than a decade. Emily would have been in her thirties had she lived.

"Thank God," she said laying fluttering hands on her chest. "How old was she? You said you were something bad that happened. What was that?"

"I have a sister. Zoe. Zoe Andreis."

Gemma's brow furrowed deeply. "The comic strip artist? It's called…Wanderlust?"

"One and the same," he said, both surprised and not that she'd heard of his sister. She was probably kind of famous in her own way.

"So you have a sister," Gemma prompted.

"Who's not speaking to me."

"Giovanni would say something like 'you're beating around the bush.'"

"Who's Giovanni?" He needed a field guide to her entourage.

Gemma turned pink in deep contrast with her hair. "Someone I talk to. Lives close by. He's got a wife."

He spun around in the chair to fully face Gemma. Once and for all face the past that he tried like hell to put behind him. He knew if he started this story, he wouldn't be able to stop. It had to be done in one fell swoop, like he was at the podium during an AA meeting. So he took a fortifying breath and plunged in. Images of the past filled his mind as though twelve years ago was only twelve minutes ago.

"Can you walk in those shoes?" he had asked his little sister, Zoe, and her friend Emily Little. The shoes in question were as pointy as a witch's hat everywhere: at their tip, at their heel. Despite their nodding, he gave them five minutes before they cried mercy, ten tops.

"Do it all the time in the city. If we can walk in New York, it shouldn't be a problem where everyone drives," Emily said laughing and doing a little dance in the witch shoes.

When he'd said his goodbyes to Zoe on her way to art school, he'd told her he wouldn't miss the perfume and makeup nor the clothes he could never figure out how to fold when they came out of the laundry. But the truth was he had missed all of it. More than he'd thought possible. After their mom, Iris, had died, Zoe was the only one who shared most of the memories of their mother. With her gone, and him out in California, it was in some ways as if their whole life in Chicago had ceased to exist. It was good to have her here as a reminder of all that had come before he was in Los Angeles, and she three thousand miles away in New York City.

"You look fab," Emily said, pointing to his sister, who was putting the final touches on…an outfit of some kind.

"Is that all?" he asked, pointing to the acres of bare leg Zoe was showing. He scanned the clothes draped on every surface of the guest room. Surely, there was more to her outfit than the scraps of fabric she wore.

"What?" She looked down as if to check to make sure she was fully dressed. "I have on a top, skirt, and shoes."

If you could call it that. The "top" consisted of a hand-kerchief's worth of fabric attached to some kind of metal loop around her neck. The skirt looked more like a wide belt with some kind of fluttery bottom than something the Catholic Church would condone. Then there were the shoes, the mirror image of Emily's, that could probably punch a hole in the wall with either the heel or the toe.

"You look stunning," Emily said in awe. "I wish I was as tall as you, Zo, so I could carry it off."

Adonis bit the inside of his cheeks. Maybe if it had been a sub-zero Chicago winter he'd have said something more. But both he and his father had lost the "you're half naked" fight one too many times for him to even try.

"Can you zip this?" Emily asked, turning her bare back to Adonis.

The upside of having a sister is that her friends some-times treated him like wallpaper. That was all good. He willed himself to keep it in check as he zipped the stop-light red top into place. Zoe's friend turned and looked into the full-length mirror, adjusting the paper-thin striped skirt across her hips.

"Where are you going?" he asked. Not that girls had a hard time finding something to do in Los Angeles. But on their first night in town, he was curious.

"We met some guys on the plane. Said there's a frat party out in Malibu that we should try," Emily answered. "Going to make use of the extra three hours of daylight."

"Malibu?" The city some twenty miles northwest of Los Angeles proper was quite a drive.

"Dad said I could borrow the truck. Figure we'd drive up. If it's a bust, we'll get sushi or go to that seafood dive on the beach you took me to last time I was in town," Zoe said.

"How about I drive?" he found himself asking, even though spending more than five minutes with frat guys would have been the dead-last choice of how he'd prefer to spend a Saturday night.

A look of some kind passed between his sister and her friend. Finally, they shrugged. "Sure," Zoe said. She tossed him their father's car keys.

He tossed them back. "Nah, I'll take my truck," he said.

Five minutes later, they were out on the street getting into the truck.

"This is very yellow," Emily said of his outsized SUV.

"Shh," Zoe said, putting an exaggerated finger to her lips. "He loves this truck like a girlfriend."

Emily laughed and swung into the front seat. His sister stretched her long legs along the back seat and off he drove. Loud music and rolled-down windows accompanied them all the way from Mid City to Malibu.

Zoe flipped open her phone and pointed to a nondescript house along the beach.

"This is the Sigma house party," she said.

"What's the plan?" he asked. Whenever he and his sister went out, they had an unspoken agreement to bail if either one of them was done.

"You know what? I'll drive back," Zoe volunteered. "You haven't really had the full college experience. You should have fun. Mingle with some girls. I'll give the signal if I'm ready."

"What's the signal?" Emily asked, looking between the back and driver's seat as Adonis squeezed his truck, with the grille guard extending its length, between a couple of luxury German convertibles, their bright leather interiors gleaming in the setting sun.

He and Zoe laughed a good long time before he turned off the car.

"Don't get it," Emily sing-songed from her perch in the passenger seat.

"Rotolo," they said in unison before a fit of laughter caught them again.

"Still not getting it," Emily said as they walked along the skinny path between cars and houses.

"It's just bad Italian," Zoe said. She flipped her phone open and closed, then pointed at a light gray house.

Hands outstretched, Adonis was sure to cut as wide a swath as possible for the girls. He didn't want an errant bougainvillea or agave plant to snag what little clothing they had on.

Red plastic cups were thrust in their hands the minute they walked into the open entry door and gave their names. After Zoe ditched her punch, he drank deeply from his own. The house, they found out, had been rented by a couple of guys. He couldn't imagine such a thing back in Chicago, laying out tens of thousands of dollars for a place to play loud music and drink underage.

Three hours later, he was taking back that thought. It was good to be rich. He'd switched from punch to tequila shots with a couple of the frat guys. They thought him being a carpenter, working with his father and uncle, was way cooler than majoring in business or marketing. He kind of had to agree with that as he licked salt and lime from his hands and lips.

BLEARY-EYED, ADONIS' buzz cleared for a moment and he realized he'd lost track of his charges.

"Anyone seen Zoe or Emily?" he asked of the three guys sitting on tall stools around the marble kitchen island.

"Who's that?" one asked.

Another elbowed his fraternity brother. "One chick in that scorching red top with her tits spilling out. The other had legs up to her ears and a skirt the size of a bandage."

"Yeah, new blood. Think they're getting the Colton Wilbanks treatment."

The laughter around the counter wasn't so friendly. Set his teeth on edge, actually.

"Colton?" He bit back the part about one of the girls being his not-so-little sister.

"He's the one who made this party happen. Kind of likes a door fee from each girl."

Laughter rippled through the assembled group. He didn't know if the tequila was making him paranoid, or if it was the shifty eyes from each guy, but he pushed back his stool.

"Gotta take a piss," he said. That was at least partly true. Instead of using the open powder room downstairs or the toilet off the poolroom, he wound his way up the steel-wrapped teak stairs. He followed the hooting laughter and peeked his head in an open bedroom door.

What he saw stopped him in his tracks.

Zoe and Emily were lolling on the bed looking a lot more than drunk. Four or five guys had their phones lifted, snapping pictures of themselves posing with each girl.

He pulled his head out and sized up the situation as best he could with his brain muddled by fermented cactus juice.

He wasn't a wizened eighty-year-old, but he'd been around the block often enough to know he had about ten minutes to get his sister and her friend out before the whole thing went south. He'd never seen any good come of a group of boys, drugs, and alcohol.

After he relieved himself, he did a quick survey of the house. It was fairly new construction. He looked up at the ceiling. Sprinklers. The house had residential sprinklers.

He tried to plow through regulations with his jumbled mind. Sometime in the last few years, new construction was required to have sprinklers and fire alarms. The kind usually installed only on commercial buildings. But with waves of brush fires and the threat of drought, city planners thought them necessary for homes.

Malibu wasn't in the city of Los Angeles. Could be a county regulation though. Or this place could be in some unincorporated area.

More laughter erupted. He didn't like his chances on taking on a whole frat. He was far from a movie superhero or martial artist, taking on dozens of men at a time and winning.

He pounded down the stairs, going for the long shot.

"Hey, carpenter man, where you going?"

"Might have to hurl," he threw over his shoulder.

On the side of the house, between tightly packed bushes, there it was.

The shiny red box had a thin plastic shield. With a pocketknife from his cargo pants, he pried open the cover and pulled the handle.

An internal alarm system screeched in warning.

It only took the Sigma brothers a minute to start running from the three-story beach house.

He shouldered his way back up the stairs to the bedroom he'd glimpsed earlier. Abandoned, the girls lay on the bed looking half dazed. Trust the Sigma brothers to be the kind of assholes to leave the girls behind to burn up in a fire. Even if the fire was pretend.

Grabbing both by the upper arms, he half lifted, half dragged them from the house. Instead of running toward the beach like the rest of the partygoers, he got them to his car. After he shoved the girls into the back seat, he got in the truck.

He flexed and unflexed his fingers in front of his eyes, watching them blur and clear. Adonis did his best to assess whether he was too drunk to drive. When he looked back at the house, he decided it didn't matter. He was driving.

No way was he going back to that disaster. In a minute an armed alarm company, or police, or firefighters, or all three would be there. Having his sister busted for underage drinking would probably fuck up her college plans. He wanted her to be able to fulfill her dream of finishing art school and doing something with her life.

Would be kind of hard to do that with a record. And if she'd been roofied, like he suspected, she would probably have a hard time even appearing to be sober. Nope. Back at that sand-colored, stuccoed palace lie disaster.

Emily and Zoe needed to get home, get sobered up, have a big breakfast burrito and get their asses on a plane back to New York City in a few days. The complicated math of number of shots versus his two hundred pounds failed him. Jamming his keys in the ignition, he backed up. The crunch of rubber on metal sobered him right quick.

He jumped from the SUV to find he'd crumpled the front end of a Mercedes. Not proud of what he was about to do, he got back in the car and carefully eased onto the Pacific Coast Highway just in time to see emergency vehicles screaming toward him from the opposite direction.

Safe from whatever consequences were coming the way of the Sigma brothers, he focused on driving. Every brain cell he had, he tuned into turning the steering wheel to follow the curves of the road, taking great care to avoid the bright headlamps that kept swerving around him. The traffic in front of him was getting complicated, though. He knew he needed to get off the One and onto the Ten. One turn, and he'd be at least halfway home. But the signs in California still confused him. They seemed to come up only seconds before a driver needed to make a quick decision. And he was in no state to make a quick decision.

Instead of trying to figure out the bridge from beach to street, he got off and wandered through Santa Monica until he found Pico Boulevard. That was an east-west street that would take him to La Brea.

Yep.

That should do it. He worked the pedals as carefully as he would his table saw. He wasn't quick enough, though. At the corner of Centinela, a car whipped out of a parking lot or off the freeway, he couldn't quite tell. One minute he was driving, the next he was jerking the wheel hard to avoid a collision.

He didn't collide with the car. For a few seconds, relief replaced the adrenaline that had rushed through his system.

Then, inexplicably, the truck was spinning, rolling over. What was up was down. The sound of crushing metal and shattering glass filled his ears.

Then there was silence.

What little control he had was lost. Vomit erupted from him and sprayed its foul texture and smell everywhere. The night's family spaghetti dinner spewing blood red. He crawled out of the open window, glass and metal cutting him everywhere.

He ignored the stinging flesh. Cars could catch on fire. He'd filled the gas tank before the drive. Twenty-plus gallons of fuel was ass over teakettle above them. A Molotov cocktail waiting to ignite.

Zoe.

Emily.

His sister's eyes, still dazed, met his. She wasn't belted in and it was easy enough to pull her from the hole where the truck's back window had been. He dragged her to the curb and propped her up next to a light post. Leaning down again, he peered in the car, but it was empty.

No sign of Emily.

He plumbed the depths of his brain. This made absolute zero sense. There were three people in the car. Three minus two was one. *That* math he could do. Where in the hell had the girl in the bright red top gone?

Lights blinded him and sirens deafened him before he could figure out a logical answer to the missing girl puzzle.

"Hey, over here," a bystander called out. He followed the voice and the movement of firefighters.

Emily.

Her body lay prone. The skirt she'd created with a single brooch holding together fabric was long gone, exposing white cotton underwear that glowed in the orange streetlights. She wasn't moving.

Despite the sudden onset of dread, he placed one foot in front of the other, gaining speed with each step. He'd have run if a steely arm hadn't come out and stopped his forward momentum.

"You're bleeding," the voice said.

"What happened to Emily?" The sound of his own voice was a croak.

"There's nothing you can do. Our guys are on the scene. Were you the driver?"

Ignoring the man holding his arm, he stared at the group of men in reflective fluorescent-green uniforms surrounding Zoe's friend. The heads of three different uniformed men shook from side to side in unison. A fourth man jumped from the truck, a sheet in his hand. He shook it out. The fabric billowed a second before carefully arranging itself over Emily. What had been Emily.

All the confusion faded and in its place was stark reality.

"Is she...dead?" he asked, holding out stupid hope that what he was seeing wasn't true.

"I'm going to need you to step over here, sir."

"Answer me!"

"Sir." The uniformed man's voice had gone from soft to stern. Before he could answer the question, another grabbed his arm in a take-no-prisoners attitude and hauled him to the bank of cars, their light bars spinning beacons of light into the night sky.

What seemed like a second later, he was in the back of a police car, speeding away from what was left of his truck, his sister, and Emily.

"Was your sister okay?" Gemma asked, bringing him back to the present.

He tried to guess what she was thinking. Condemnation. Disgust. Horror. He didn't want Gemma Hart to matter. What she thought of him to matter. But it did, quite a lot.

She'd been a victim.

He'd been a perpetrator.

She needed to forgive. He needed forgiveness, but he was making no bones about it being the same. He looked at her, realized she was waiting for an answer. Waiting to find out what other punishment had been meted out.

Other than the torture of living with what he'd done, there'd been none.

FOURTEEN

Gemma

Adonis had hunched over, folding into himself like he was cold and shivering in the back of that cop car, instead of warm and safe in a house high atop Malibu's cliffs.

"She was fine. More shaken up than anything. I'm not sure how much she remembers. The frat guys had definitely slipped her something, blood tests showed. Dad picked her up at the hospital after he left me at the jail."

"Jail?" The Americans did love punishment and prison. She should have guessed he'd end up there, for killing someone.

"I failed the sobriety test. I was a point one-oh-three."

A drink-drive offense, she calculated in her head. But what about the girl?

"And Emily?" she asked.

He realized he'd never quite communicated what he'd seen with certainty. "Dead on impact with Pico Boulevard. The collision of her skull and spine on the cold, hard pavement had ended her life. No seat belt plus ejection from the SUV was a formula for death. No matter how many times I've replayed the events, everything went wrong. Everything."

"What happened after that?"

"I spent two years at the bottom of a tequila bottle. I woke up most days feeling no better than the worm. God knows how horrible I was to my friends and family. I don't actually have any friends from before," he admitted.

"My dad sold his half of the business to his brother, Alessandro, liquidated his savings paying for a defense attorney. Guy kept me out of jail. Time served, plus community service. Took me a couple of years to get my license back."

"That was it?" Gemma asked, shocked at such a light sentence. Surely death added up to more than that.

"Plus a lifetime of guilt. Yeah, that was it," he answered.

"I'm sorry. I don't know what else to say." Gemma looked everywhere but at him while she processed what he'd shared. Of all the things that were possible, drinking and death hadn't crossed her mind. Not once.

With what looked like a ton of effort, Adonis plastered a half-smile on his face. She had to appreciate the effort. She too wanted to do whatever she could to break the tension, to bring them back to where they'd been a few days earlier when their time hadn't been clouded by truth and tragedy.

"It's not my opening with women. Hi, I have all my hair, teeth, and a business, but a manslaughter in my past."

"That's not funny," she said after his lame attempt at humor fell as flat as a pancake.

"I know. Nothing about it is good or funny. There is no silver lining."

"How did your sister handle it?" she asked. He hadn't been the only one to survive that night.

"I don't know. We don't speak," he said, his tone clipped.

"About the accident?"

"About anything. She went back to school then moved abroad for ten years."

"Her comic is about her life abroad. She made that her entire life," Gemma said, fitting the pieces of a puzzle together. That she could understand, doing whatever you could to cope. Running away. She'd run away, not as far, for certain, but away from all those who would condemn her. From her agent and aunt and all those who reminded her of what she wanted to forget.

"Until now," Adonis was saying. "She came back a few months ago after Dad collapsed in your living room."

"Right. God, I was so stupid about that." Gemma could feel heat stealing up her face. Panic about exposing her location to potential stalkery fans had clouded her judgment big time. Imagining that turning out like Adonis' bad call scared the spit out of her. She needed to apologize to Dominic about that once and for all. "Sorry. So Zoe, that's her name right, she and you never got past this?"

"She blames me. I blame myself."

"Does she know the whole story? The Colton bloke who was probably going to take advantage of her. The fire stuff. All of that?" She couldn't imagine Zoe not forgiving her brother if she knew the lengths he'd gone through to spare her from harm, even as he'd put her in harm's way.

"No." He shook his head vehemently. "She knows nothing. She thinks I was being a chauvinist pig for not trusting her to drive, for taking the keys."

"But she was drugged."

"She doesn't remember any of that. Doctors say trauma blocked out most of that night. Brain self-defense mechanism. I know it's true for me. I don't remember much after that night and two years later."

"Gosh, you've both suffered so much."

"In her mind, she had a little punch that wasn't spiked, then I did the caveman big brother thing and wrestled them home, killing her best friend along the way."

"Are you going to ever tell her the entire story?"

"What's the point, Gemma? It doesn't make me any less guilty for doing what I did. Doesn't make Emily any less dead."

Gemma's phone beeped. After she pulled the smartphone from her pocket, she looked at it like it was an alien being landed on Earth. Giovanni. She'd never forgotten about her appointment before. Usually she sat in the house tapping her foot until she could get in her car and make the drive south.

"I've got to go," she said. Suddenly she moved around the room, trying to remember where she'd last left her keys, dog leash, and the rest of it.

"Go? Go where?" he asked, glancing from the computer monitor, she and O'Bryan frozen onscreen, to his watch, to her, and back toward the screen again.

She stepped forward and slipped her hand around the back of the monitor until she found the button to turn off the onscreen image of her—naked, stupid, naïve. "Appointment."

She could see he didn't believe her. Thought she was running away from the hard stuff. Maybe she was, though she'd say she was running toward the harder stuff.

"So…"

"I'll see you in the morning. Cabinets, yeah. Sounds like it will be a big day or two. Then after that they measure for the stone, right?"

She might not be an expert at relationships, but she was becoming quite knowledgeable about home renovation project management. But like learning fencing or learning to play violin—like she'd done for movies—it wasn't a skill she was likely to need again.

Gemma wanted to answer the question in his eyes, but couldn't. She had no idea what they were to each other, where all this honesty left them. Lovers? Friends? Something more? A lot less?

♥

"YOU SLEPT WITH YOUR CONTRACTOR?" Giovanni said to her forty-five minutes later.

"I didn't show up without an appointment," she grudgingly acknowledged, hoping that would deflect him from Adonis. She did and didn't want to talk about him at the same time. "I can be taught."

"Did you agree on parameters?" Giovanni persisted.

"What do you mean, parameters? We used protection, if that's what you're worried about. I won't show up pregnant and further toss my career in the loo."

"I'm probably the only person on Earth not worried about your career, Gemma. But I don't know if we have time to play the avoidance game today. If you want to do the hard work, you're going to have to dig deep."

She turned her head and looked at his shelving. The inset halogen lights were a nice touch. She'd have to review her own plans to make sure she'd remembered to include that. They'd set off the Oscars, Golden Globes, and her one SAG award and bound scripts pretty nicely. Her future might be up in the air, but she did have some past achievements that were worth honoring.

"What does that mean?" she finally asked, turning back to face her therapist head-on.

"It means, you can't walk into my office, tell me you've managed to sleep with this guy you've targeted, the first man you've talked about other than Andrew O'Bryan, then discuss inappropriate boundaries and whether or not you'll be working on a film in the next six months. We need to start with the most immediate and intimate."

"Fine." Gemma clasped and unclasped her hands. Thought about buffing her nails when she got home. Considered her pedicure. Thought about whether Sylvester could find someone to do a massage at her house since her old therapist didn't drive north of Beverly Hills.

"Gemma?"

Giovanni didn't say the clock was ticking, but he might as well have.

"He wasn't an asshole," she started. Thought better of it. Took a course correction. "I mean, he was nice."

"Did you tell him you intended it to be a one-night

stand kind of thing?" Giovanni asked. He was leaning forward, his brown eyes intense.

Now she remembered, parameters. She was supposed to let people know what she was looking for from a relationship. She was supposed to speak her mind and not let herself be railroaded by someone else's agenda. She'd forgotten all that in the heat of the moment. Pleasure had obliterated rational thought.

She shook her head. "It kind of happened again today," she admitted. "So maybe two-night stand?"

"Most people, Gemma. Most people can handle a new and budding relationship. As a matter of fact, they're probably looking for it. Are you? We've talked a little about trust, and you don't have much. If you haven't told him that you only want something very casual and very secret, he may not know that. His expectations may be very different from yours."

"Who *hasn't* violated my trust?" she asked. Adonis seemed sincere, but she did half expect her face to be plastered on one of the newsstand rags, or online next to a snap of her builder. Maybe not today or tomorrow, but a month from now when her project ended.

"I haven't."

"It's your job. You're probably required by law to keep secrets. Plus, everyone I've met in the last few years has been papered over by NDAs." One violation and she'd probably own Giovanni's house. Not that she'd take the action threatened in the agreement, but she didn't think it had zero effect on keeping people in line. Which is why she had Sylvester deliver one to every single person she talked to, from builder to house cleaner.

"It is my job, Gemma. But that hasn't stopped a lot of people in this town from talking. The tabloids operate on the very notion of violation of trust. Do you trust your contractor?"

"I trust Adonis." She smiled at *his* quick smile. Then they both laughed. Tension eased in the room.

"Where's he from?" Giovanni asked. For just a moment, Gemma's breathing eased. With Giovanni's voice so friendly, she could pretend that he was a friend and they were gabbing about her new man. Not like she was a woman past thirty whose emotional growth was stunted.

"Chicago. Has the accent."

"How long has he been out here?"

"Fifteen years, maybe? His whole family left and came here after he graduated high school."

"Why California?"

"Maybe to run the construction business? I don't know."

"These are the kinds of facts people share about themselves when they're starting a relationship, Gemma. Usually before they jump into bed together."

"I wasn't planning on getting into a relationship," she countered. "I'm not sure I even want one. My goal was to try to get my own stuff together, you know. Figure out my career. Try to make friends. Figure out if I'm ready to deal with my aunt's betrayal. Romance was not, is not, in the picture."

"Then why did you sleep with him again?"

"I shagged him because I'm human and he was willing. And God forgive me, he's a total Adonis."

"What is he expecting? You know I'm not an advice giver. I'm not your…how did you refer to her?"

"Agony aunt."

"Right. I love that way more than shag, snog, or spanner. Anyway. I'm not your agony aunt, but please hear me on this. Before you see him again, or sleep with him, or whatever, you've got to think about what you want from him, a causal affair that ends when your tile is installed, or something more."

"I didn't think men needed those kinds of guidelines. I thought they were just happy to get a leg over."

"I'm not talking about him, Gemma. I'm talking about you. You've been hurt, you've been betrayed, you've been violated. In order for that not to happen again, you'll need to decide what you want. It's not up to anyone but you."

"Well that's easy," she said, heaping her voice with tons of sarcasm.

"I told you when we started a few months ago, that none of this was going to be easy."

"I'm not a good candidate for a relationship, anyway."

"Why?" Giovanni's face was genuinely perplexed. As if she weren't a Pandora's box of crazy better kept sealed tight than unleashed on the unsuspecting.

"For the reasons you said today. For the reasons you said in June. Because I don't leave the house. Because I don't trust anyone. Because he's an alcoholic."

"Whoa. Back up. He's in recovery?"

"That's what he says. I offered him a sherry. He turned me down."

Giovanni rubbed his head like she made migraines to order. "How many years?"

"Ten. Twelve, maybe. He was in his twenties."

"That's young to already have given up alcohol. Did he say what the catalyst was?"

"I'm just going to say this. Because it's quite horrible. Brace yourself." Giovanni nodded, so she blurted it out as fast as she could, as if fast speech would lessen the impact. "He killed someone in a drunk-driving accident. Someone in his own car."

Silence permeated the room for a good minute while they both absorbed the information, her for a second time, Giovanni for the first.

As if the silence were a person who stole into the room, Granger lifted his head and sniffed the air. His ID and rabies tags jingled like out-of-tune bells.

"And how do you feel about that?" Giovanni finally asked.

"Seriously? That's the question you have?" She'd made fun of just that question during their first session. He'd promised then to try not to ask it.

"Just because it's a cliché doesn't mean it's not an honest question."

"He told me all of ten minutes ago. That's a lot to process. I walked out of the door on that conversation and drove down here to see you."

"You could have canceled, Gemma."

"It was easier coming here and subjecting myself to your questions than talking to him. What in the hell was I going to say? I'd showed him the sex tape. I'd offered him sherry. That was all I was prepared to deal with today. But I went on about how O'Bryan's sobriety was bullshit and Adonis started defending the guy."

163

"Back up, Gemma. First things first. You showed him the tape?"

"After that first time, we, you know...Sylvester asked him if I was as good as the tape."

"Jesus, Gemma. Sylvester said that?"

"He's a guy. That's how they act."

"Not all guys act like that. Why show him the tape, though? Normally sexual history isn't something partners discuss outright. We discussed that particular boundary if you remember."

"He asked if I'd been honest about my sexual history. He didn't outright call me a liar, but that was the implication. I wanted him to know it was more Bill Clinton and less Kim Kardashian."

She bent down and petted the dog. She looked out the window. She wondered where Giovanni's wife kept her awards. Flicking a glance at her therapist under her lashes, she watched as he fit together the puzzle pieces.

"Oh, Gemma." It wasn't so much him figuring out her most embarrassing secret, it was the sympathy and sorrow that laced his voice. As if she were a bigger freak than he'd ever thought.

"Please, not the one-man pity party. I've won two Oscars. Getting my SAG card was about a thousand times easier than getting a man interested in me for something other than what I could do for his career."

"Here are your three questions," he said, not addressing her admission. Instead, he moved on to their usual end-of-session wrap-up. "Your homework is to really dig deep and answer, okay?"

She nodded, pulling out the leather-bound journal

she'd ordered online. The one with the brass comedy and tragedy masks affixed. The one that was supposed to help her fix all that had gone wrong in her life.

"Decide where you're going to go. Enough with hiding out. Be safe, but go somewhere, anywhere. Decide if you want a relationship. Decide if you want any kind of relationship with Adonis, because what he's laid out is the kind of thing that would be a deal breaker for a lot of people. You have to decide if it's a deal breaker for you."

Quickly, she scribbled down his three questions, which had morphed into an entire project that would make her brain nearly explode.

"Picking a good script would be easier than this," she said, closing the leather and snicking the hook into the clasp.

"A good script is a temporary fix, Gemma. Living your best life is permanent."

FIFTEEN

Dominic

Dominic double-checked his watch against the digital display in the truck. Ten thirty was safely inside the window. Bridget had left a message saying she would be out today with some friends until well after lunch.

Glancing in the back of the truck's cab, he checked his supplies. A small can of paint would finish the laundry room. The tube of caulk and plumber's tape should make short work of the sink and vanity installation. He was pretty sure he'd seen the new light fixture in a box wedged between the bathroom and coat closet doors.

In and out in two hours. Shouldn't take him a minute more. Paint and caulk did not venture into the category of unforeseen circumstances — the contractor's enemy.

He let himself into the back door.

The smell assaulted him first. Pumpkin spice mingled with chicken. He was a better cook, but Bridget's food reminded him of Chicago, a warm, wholesome homecoming. The smells wafting through the house made him nostalgic for all the stupid hopes he'd built up about them having a future, about him being ready to try again. He'd thought she was too. But like some silly twenty-year-old who didn't know any better, he'd been useful, then summarily discarded.

Patched roof, new laundry room shelving, and an updated powder room had been the price of his hopes. He'd sold himself far too cheap.

Shaking his head at his own stupidity, he surveyed the small laundry room. Getting out the small roller, Dominic worked briskly to hide scuff marks he'd made when he'd dragged the bulky washer and dryer back inside.

He stepped back to assess his work. It was good. Everything looked damned near perfect. He rinsed the paint in the utility sink then headed to the bathroom.

He was working his smoothing tool over the caulk where the new sink rested against the wall when a door opened somewhere in the house. The creak of an unoiled hinge nearly had him pissing himself.

He gripped the trigger of the caulk gun in fear, squeezing a thick bead into the bowl of the sink.

Who in the hell was in the house? He hadn't locked the back door, but the Valley wasn't exactly Chicago's South Side. He couldn't think of anyone who'd walk in the door without knocking. That said, he didn't exactly know any of Bridget's friends.

One of Bridget's sons, maybe?

A burglar?

He looked from the tool in his right hand and the small plastic triangle, no bigger than a credit card, in the left. As much as he and that Cameron Becker had bumped heads all those months ago when Bridget had been nursing him back to health, an LAPD officer would be welcome right now.

Sucking in breath, puffing out his chest, and pulling himself up to his full sixty-seven inches of height, he stormed out the door.

"I'm not alone! Killer, my pit bull, is waiting in the backyard," he yelled toward the intruder.

"You got a dog?"

It was Bridget. No Cameron. No serial killer.

Huffing out breath and returning to normal size, Dominic came into the entranceway and Bridget came fully into view.

"No, I don't have a dog. What are you doing here?"

"Now what kind of greeting is that? This, as you may recall, is my house. I live here. I can come and go as I please," she said, her tone a sharp reprimand.

"Yes, of course. It's your house, Bridget. I'd do well to remember that. We agreed that I would finish up here today. You were going to 'do lunch' with some of your lady friends. We talked by e-mail."

"Right. Forgot about that. I was at the store," she said, holding up bags with a familiar red-and-white logo.

"Let me get out of your hair," he said. He walked back to the small bathroom. He scraped the caulk from the sink, wishing he could scrape away his feelings for Bridget. But the woman had gotten under his skin and it wasn't so easily done.

He checked the drawers in the vanity. They moved smoothly on their rollers. The inserts were firmly fixed. The knobs attached securely. Leaning down, he packed up his tools in the Wynne Avenue house for the last time.

After today, he probably wouldn't see Bridget again. He'd live his life. She would live out hers.

Standing, he took a deep breath. He'd learned a very important lesson in the last few months he and Bridget had gone out. He'd learned that he could love again. Maybe she couldn't. But he could. And that had to be enough.

Invigorated, he gathered up the little bits of plastic and cardboard that had held the drawers closed.

He nearly knocked Bridget over when he came to the door. "You have a whole three-bedroom house. Why are you standing here?"

"I wanted to thank you."

"For..." He could think of a couple of things she might be thankful for, and one of them wasn't construction. *He'd* certainly been thankful that night. He'd almost forgotten how much fun it could be with a woman in bed. Especially when the issue of birth control stopped being relevant. They might not be as flexible as the twenty-something crowd, but it had been surprisingly sexy nonetheless.

"Your work on the house. If there's any way I could pay you back, I would."

"It was a favor. I'm always happy to do those for friends. I know you don't want anything more, but I hope we can at least be friends," he said, his words a peace offering. He wasn't a tit-for-tat guy. Had never been. She'd been in a bind. He'd helped her out. Certainly nothing for him to be resentful about. "We're good," he said, imitating the young guy from the paint store.

"You hungry for lunch?" she asked, not taking a step back to let him out of the room.

"Didn't you already eat?"

"My friends were busy. Sophie got them tickets to see *The Price is Right.*"

"You didn't want to go?" he asked. He certainly wasn't into game shows, but it was probably fun for the middle-aged crowd.

"I'm too old to stand outside of CBS for hours waiting in line to win a car I don't need or a trip I won't take or a washer-dryer when I already have one."

As if on cue, his traitorous stomach rumbled. "If lunch wouldn't be too much trouble…"

"It's never trouble, Dominic. It's the least I can do. Come on out. Have a seat."

Leaving his tools by the front door, he headed to the dining room. He sat at the table, set now with a harvest-theme tablecloth and napkins. Multicolored fall leaves fanned out from the placemat. He traced their contours, remembering how much he and the kids had loved that season before the cold, wind, and lake-effect snow kept them all indoors for five months, more days than not.

Bridget came back, platter of roast chicken and vegetables in one hand, dinner rolls in the other.

"Were you expecting company?" He half stood as he asked the question, relieving her of the bread. "I can get my stuff. I didn't mean to crash your party."

"I wasn't expecting anyone other than you, Dominic."

He sat back down, confusion fogging his mind. The smell of roasted chicken triggered something in his brain, and his stomach rumbled again. Maybe it was the hunger causing all the confusion. Shouldn't have skipped breakfast, but he'd been eager to get over here and get the last of the work done before Bridget came home.

"I may not remember a lot," she said, laying a serving spoon and carving knife on the table, "but I do still believe that a way to a man's heart is through his stomach."

His heart stopped and his stomach left his insides. Without either, he was having a hard time breathing.

Bridget went in the kitchen, came back with a pumpkin pie. After she deposited it on a trivet, she hovered around him, her oven mitts fluttering like leaves in a stiff Chicago wind.

"Bridget, sit down. You're driving me nuts with all this walking around."

As if the chair were the enemy, she bent her knees slowly, carefully, only then sliding her butt onto half of the seat. The leg that wasn't on the chair jiggled. In an instant, she was up again. Lifting the serving spoon, she put a chicken leg and a medley of roasted vegetables on his plate.

He sank a fork into a sweet potato and bit into it. The sweet and salty combination of chicken juices and sugary potato was divine.

"It's good. You've outdone yourself. Are you going to eat?"

A sliver of breast and a few potatoes appeared on her plate. She stood; pouring drinks, straightening his napkin, then did a half-stand, half-crouch.

"Quit hovering. Sit down and tell me why you'd want to make a way to my heart. A couple of weeks ago, I think you said that it wasn't on. I was just about to ask Nicki to set me up on one of those dating sites. The kids say that an old man like me will be in high demand."

"I don't want you to sign up for anything."

"Why not, Bridget? Why shouldn't I sign up for Our Time or Senior People Meet?"

"God, those sound like we're on the verge of death. I'm still offended by the free AARP card that came in the mail."

"I think it's time I use the computer in my shed for more than e-mailing clients and checking on supplies," he said, pressing home his point that he was ready to move forward.

"I think your girlfriend wouldn't be happy."

"Girlfriend? Last time I checked, I didn't have one of those. My spackle knife and cordless drill have been my closest companions lately."

"You're being deliberately obtuse, Dominic Andreis."

"You're not saying anything I understand, Bridget Becker."

At a standstill, they ate their meal in near silence. She disappeared for ten minutes then came back with two steaming mugs of coffee and a canister of whipped cream. Dollops were applied to slices of pie and they dug in.

Sated, Dominic sat back in his chair. Because the topic of potential girlfriends was on the table, he resisted the urge to unbutton the jeans that were just a mite too tight after all that food.

"I was thinking about divorcing my husband."

The sentence echoed in the too silent room. Her husband was long dead. He was sure of that. Her marriage must not have been as happy as she'd let on.

"But he died first?"

"In the worst way possible. One night I was lying next to him, wishing him dead. The next day, he died. It's as if my anger somehow ended his life."

"That makes absolutely no sense," he said. But it did make a kind of sense, in a sad and macabre way.

"Of course it doesn't make any sense. This is the first time I've ever said anything out loud. But that guilt has been eating away at me from the day I got the call from the Strohmeyer brewery."

"What do your kids think?"

"What do my kids think? That I had an ideal marriage. That their father's death was a tragedy from which I've never really recovered."

"Is that why you didn't make a claim for the money, death benefits or retirement or whatever was owed?"

"I have a conscience. I had to do what was right. Instead of taking the money I probably would have gotten if I'd fought for it, I worked night and day, two jobs sometimes, making sure my boys had what they needed."

"But you want to try us?"

"I married Donald because he asked. Because I didn't have confidence that anyone else would ever ask. There were good times, don't get me wrong. He loved me in his way, I think. But not in the way that I needed. I always felt I was second to whatever held his attention, work, the boys, his friends, his poker games, what have you. It was like he had a life checklist. He married me, ticked off 'wife,' and moved on to the next. I came after secure job but before ranch house."

"And now?"

"I needed time to think. I needed time to figure out if I was making the same mistake twice. If I was saying yes to you just because you'd asked."

"And what happened after you thought about it?"

"I really like you, Dominic. You're smart, funny, handy. I think you've been a great dad to your kids. That they still want to be with you says a lot."

"I thought you just wanted me for my hammer." He made his voice light, but was only half joking.

"I wish you hadn't thought that. I'm sorry about what I said to you. I kind of needed space and time and didn't know how to ask for it. You're what, only the third man I've ever slept with. I didn't take that lightly. Still don't. It shook me to the core. It was…"

"Like something out of this world."

"Yes, that," she whispered, blushing furiously. "But I'm not twenty. I didn't want to confuse my…you know… with my brain. I did that years ago. Never again."

"What does that make us?" he asked gently. Bridget had not been shy, or retiring, or the least bit scared to share her opinion. But on this, she was different, hesitant. It charmed him. Made him believe what she was saying was real. The hope he'd thought dead, burgeoned again, bubbling up like indigestion. "What—" he started to ask again.

"Don't make me say it another time."

"Come over here," he beckoned.

"Where?"

"To my side of the table."

She stood and walked around the scarred wood table, her steps tentative. When she was within reach, Dominic pulled her with a swift tug. Off her balance, she landed in his lap with an unladylike "ooof." It was the best sound he'd ever heard.

"Dominic!" Her protest wasn't more than symbolic.

"This calls for a celebration."

"Like wine or champagne? I don't have any of that."

"Nope, something even better, that's free..." Then he kissed her like a starving man, because he'd missed her, because he liked her, because he wanted to cement their future.

SIXTEEN

Adonis

"Hold on to your hammer."

It was Gemma Hart, massive mega movie star, standing in her kitchen looking at him. He didn't know which was more surreal. The fact that it was someone so famous talking to him. A face that ninety-nine percent of Americans knew better than they knew their own mothers'.

Or the fact that after what he'd revealed, she was *still* speaking to him. That she hadn't clammed up and closed off.

Or the fact that he'd been the one to take her virginity, or take her, and Mother of God, he wanted to do it again, and again. And another time after that.

So he held on to his hammer and waited for what was next.

"Do you want to go out on a date?"

Her question was wholly unexpected. Honestly, he'd thought, and maybe half wished, that she was going to ask him to quit his work and invite him back to her bedroom. This, though, was probably the second-best thing she could have said.

"Why, Gemma Hart, you don't just want me for my body?" He tried for a playful, teasing tone. The kind couples on TV used with each other. The kind he and Gemma had never used with each other. Because they weren't a couple. They were boss and contractor. Employer and employee. She hadn't asked for or offered more. But suddenly he did want more. He pushed that thought to the farthest reaches of his brain.

"I'm serious," she said.

And once he seated his hammer and screwdriver in his belt, he realized she was. Drop-dead serious. The same way she'd been the first time she's propositioned him. Only this time he was much better at reading her, knew she meant what she said, no matter how awkwardly it came out.

"Something tells me you already have something planned." He leaned against the counter and watched Gemma and Granger. The latter was scratching his shoulder with his back leg. A small cloud of white and red hair filled the air around him.

"So...I get these e-mails from the Geffen Playhouse. They mount a bunch of shows each season. Anyway, an actor I know, Jesse Jacobs, is in a play there. I bought tickets."

"A friend of yours?" He shouldn't have asked, but he couldn't resist. Sadly, he couldn't imagine Gemma with friends. She was far too reclusive to have a big gregarious group of people whom she saw regularly. He was thinking that it was possible Sylvester was her best friend. If that were true, it would be even sadder. Pulling his mind back to the present, he looked at Gemma as she spoke.

"I wouldn't exactly call him that," she said, confirming his suspicions. "We worked together on *Seventh Voyage* years ago. We haven't talked since then, but he's a really good actor. I only wish I could be half as good. I'd love to see him on stage, though."

"Do you act in theater?" he asked. She hadn't worked the entire time he or his father had been working at her house. But his experience in L.A. was that actors worked very little unless they had a television show or were at the tippy top of the actor popularity pyramid. Gemma was well known, famous, but she wasn't Meryl Streep. Maybe she was preparing for a play. It would certainly explain what she did with the hours upon hours she spent tucked upstairs with Granger.

"Never." She shook her head, dramatically killing that assumption dead. "Not my medium. I grew up in film. Stage work takes talent. A presence. A good film director, cinematographer, and editor can really make an onscreen performance better. Onstage, there's nothing between an actor and the audience. I need that buffer."

"I'm sure that isn't true," he said. Was she fishing for a compliment, or did she really not have great confidence in herself? "You have those Oscars." He wasn't an actor, but knew that there were thousands of people who would kill for that particular honor.

"God, there are probably dozens of books that ponder why Oscar movies are not the best of the best. That first one I got because I was a kid. Who doesn't love a precocious kid? The second was all politics. They snubbed the director, so four of us got statuettes as a kind of peace offering."

"So the date?" he asked before she boarded the one-person pity-party train.

"Right. Sorry. The show is at eight o'clock, if you're interested."

"Do you want to go to dinner?"

Gemma's eyes widened as if he'd suggested something as wild as going bungee jumping.

"No. I can't do a restaurant right now. It's too late to get a private room at most places. I can't be in the middle of a room. I can't finish a meal that way. Or even feel comfortable eating."

"Sorry. I didn't know," he murmured. Sounded crazy and outlandish to him. He'd probably seen his fair share of celebrities out in the "wild" and he couldn't think of a single time he'd accosted one.

"So, if we leave at seven, I think we should get there just in time to get seated and watch the show. We have to leave right afterwards, though. Okay. I know. I see your face. It's totally crazy, but it's the way I have to do things, otherwise chaos."

"Let's leave at seven then," he said.

"Wow. Great. I have to go print out tickets or get them from will call or something. Thanks. This is cool," she said, practically bounding out of the room like a child with a new toy. Granger, bone in mouth, followed behind, his tail wagging gleefully. For Granger at least, her enthusiasm was infectious.

He turned back to the work of making sure each electrical box was situated properly and affixing them with the extra-long screws he needed when clients chose a granite or tile backsplash. Adonis found himself smiling and whistling, infected as well. He couldn't remember the last time he'd looked forward to a date. And as an added bonus, she knew the worst about him and wanted to still go out with him anyway.

"Oh, God. You're going to need something to wear," Gemma said, running back into the room. "Do I need to have Sylvester send some clothes your way? What's your size? Wait, I'll get some paper."

She ran away, gone for a good ten minutes before he could get a moment to speak.

Skidding back into the room on rainbow-colored flip-flops, she said, "I've rung up my shopper. Barneys should have something they can deliver in the next couple of hours. I've used them before. They're guaranteed not to send over anything that requires instructions to put on."

"I have clothes, Gemma."

"It's no bother really." She fingered a smartphone. "If you're busy, I can figure out the size, though you're much bigger, taller, and a bit broader than most men I've worked with. But—"

"I have clothes, Gemma," he repeated.

"So...well...I know everyone practically wears track suits and singlets everywhere they go, but..."

It took a lot of effort to hide his smile. He decided to let Gemma twist in the wind a moment longer. Watch her British sensibilities get her panties in a twist.

"Why are you smiling?" she asked, finally catching on that she was missing something.

"I have clothes, Gemma." He plucked at his polyester-blend work shirt and cargo pants. "More than this. I won't embarrass you."

"No, you could never embarrass me. I wasn't saying that at all," she backpedaled. "I wouldn't want you to feel uncomfortable is all. People may stare at you more than usual."

"I have a white button-down shirt and dark slacks in the van."

"You carry a change of clothes?"

"When I have to talk to the city or county about permits and inspections, I don't go in work boots or clothes with paint on them," he said, flicking at the blue and white paint flecks on his pants from a long-ago job.

"Oh, yeah. I see. Sorry. I'll um, get Sylvester's assistant to cancel the call from the personal shopper at Barneys. I'll say it was a mix-up."

"Good idea. Now I really need to get back to this to keep on schedule. Seven."

Eight hours later, he cursed himself a thousand times a fool. He should have taken the offer of that fancy department store in Beverly Hills. He was no match for Gemma.

He felt like a sixteen-year-old boy on his way to high school prom, when he realized his girlfriend, the one who usually wore jeans and t-shirts, was really a beautiful woman in disguise.

Only there was no disguise. Gemma came down the steps in a multicolored print dress that made her skin luminous, her hair look like fire.

"You look amazing," he breathed. Unable to resist, he pulled her in. Kissed the impossibly shiny lips. They were as sweet and soft as he remembered. Maybe even more so. He used one hand to cup her downy-soft neck, the other to explore the curves of her back and bottom.

Fuck.

Is exactly what he wanted to do. Plays and theater and sitting in a plush chair for two hours be damned. He wanted to reverse what she'd done.

"God, Gemma. I want to take that dress right off you, pull the pins from your hair, kiss the lipstick from your mouth."

Gasping, she pulled back. Her eyes were glittery, feverish with the same attraction, arousal that was pooling in his belly and lower.

"I, uh, bought tickets…" she said, speaking sense.

"And to the Geffen we shall go."

In the hour it took to drive along the coast, he alternated looking though the passenger window at the waves pounding the rocks on shore. When the traffic slowed, he turned toward Gemma. She'd insisted on driving, saying the big yellow van was a bit much. That if low-key was how she was going to go—and unless it was a movie premiere, she always traveled low-key—that taxi-cab yellow was the exact opposite.

"Why don't you go out?" he asked.

"Where?"

"I don't know. L.A., even Malibu has a lot of entertainment."

"You sound like Giovanni."

"Sounds like a smart guy. I was thinking about restaurants, movies, the mall, the stuff everybody does."

"You think that I can just walk everywhere unaccosted? That not a single person would ask me for an autograph?"

"Isn't that the cost of doing business? You have a really nice house, this car, employees. All because people are fans of your work. But the pleasure of living a real life has to outweigh that small inconvenience, right?"

"Maybe. I hear that New York City is better. I've thought of living there."

He ignored that one. He wanted more time to explore whatever it was they were doing. Three thousand miles between them would make that impossible. He wanted the possibilities. Life, that had seemed to be without for so long, was suddenly looking much different.

"How do your friends feel about always having to come to your house?" he asked, continuing his probe. It probably wasn't the most artful way of going about it, but he wanted to know why Gemma was so alone. He wanted her to be less lonely.

"Friends?" Her laugh was awkward, sad. "I don't have any of those."

"You don't? How long have you lived in California?"

Gemma didn't answer, instead eyed a left turn with suspicion. In his opinion, she waited a beat too long before swinging the SUV onto Westwood Boulevard, but having a mother and sister cured him of the need to comment on her driving. Instead, he asked, "Did you learn to drive here?"

"In the States? No. I should have. I was in Berkshire for six months and my dad taught me to drive. I can navigate a mean roundabout."

"Do you have a California license?" he asked when she nearly swiped a car.

"No. Sylvester taught me how to drive on the wrong side of the road."

"How do you get on without a license?" He had to show his ID at least once a day, if not more.

"No one ever asks who I am." She turned toward him, her right eyebrow arched so high it nearly hit her hairline. "They usually tell me who I am."

Without incident, but with a lot of prayer from his side of the SUV, Gemma navigated the tight parking lot. He breathed a little sigh of relief when she popped the locks.

"The tickets are at will call," she said. He followed behind her like a lost puppy. He shouldn't criticize her driving. He was the *last* person who should probably make comments about someone's driving.

There were about twenty people milling in the small courtyard area. The theater looked like a brick and stucco house, nothing like the Pantages on Hollywood Boulevard or Chicago Theater on State Street. Nothing about this unassuming place tucked between UCLA and Westwood's high-rise corridor of doctors' offices and luxury apartments screamed live theater.

"It's over there," he said, pointing to a short line of a few couples, and landed a hand at Gemma's back. The smile she flashed was quick and grateful.

The noise level in the courtyard became…weird was the only way to describe it. First the noise level rose, then a hush and all eyes turned first on Gemma, then skimmed over him, then returned to Gemma. Then the voices rose again. A few phones poised in vertical testament to their dual use as cameras were lifted. LED lights flashed and dimmed over a few seconds.

He looked at the people taking pictures of her and him like they were a pair of endangered rhinoceros at the zoo, then at Gemma. She was either completely unaware or studiously avoiding every look and stare. It was a unique skill how she didn't make eye contact with anyone while not looking like she was doing it.

When it was their turn at the window, he leaned down as Gemma approached, ready to answer the cashier's questions.

"I'm—"

Before Gemma could get more than a single word in, the clerk gushed. "Gemma Hart! Yes. It's you. My gosh! I hope you enjoy the show tonight. Here are your tickets," the woman said, nearly breathless, pushing a small envelope across the counter. "We'll have someone to assist you in a moment."

Gemma slipped the two tickets from the small paper sheath. She turned them toward her at such an angle that both she and Adonis could read the words. Seat numbers AAA 101, AAA 102 and AAA 103 were printed in bold black type.

"Thanks," Gemma said. "I think we shouldn't have any problems—"

Before she could finish the sentence, an usher was at their side, escorting them through the crowd and showing them not to a row or aisle, but right to their seats. They were in the first row. She'd reserved a seat on the aisle and the two next to it.

"Cheers, mate," Gemma said to the usher.

The man seemed hesitant to take his leave. While he hovered, inquiring about the empty seat, another man joined them, pushing a program and an extra stack of flyers their way.

Graciously, Gemma accepted them, stashing them in a sturdy square purse then taking the seat on the aisle. Adonis took the seat next to her and watched the ushers fade as a crush of people stood tapping their feet by the theater doors.

"I always sit on the aisle, in the first row," she said.

The why question almost escaped his lips before it became obvious. It was the seat that made staring at his date the most difficult.

"No one can turn around and look at you."

"You catch on quickly. Nothing is more disrespectful to actors than turning to watch someone in the crowd have their back to you half the show."

Right at show time, the lights flickered then dimmed, and the crowd noise quieted. An announcement about cell phones and picture taking came across a loudspeaker. He flicked off his cell phone then watched as the actors came upon a stage set up like an urban backyard.

The first act of the play—which on the surface was about a family barbecue, but was really more about acceptance—moved quickly. The lessons about love and family hit him a little too close and a little too hard.

He vowed right then to do his damnedest to make up with his sister. He only had the one, and they both needed to forgive each other and get past their mistakes. He watched the play with half his brain.

Once that was settled in his mind, the other half of his

brain inevitably focused on Gemma. It was the first time he'd ever seen her out of her element. Her face was flushed, and her laugh hearty. She looked like she was having a great time. He would do his best to take her to as many places as their short time together would allow.

Gemma Hart out in the world was a beautiful thing.

"Shit," Gemma hissed when the curtain came down, signaling the end of the first act.

"What?"

"I have to pee."

He laughed in spite of her serious tone. "That's a national crisis?"

"Have you ever seen a smartphone edging in from the stall next to you?"

He tried to take in the bizarreness of that. Had no personal experience where he could slot in such an invasion of privacy. "Can't say that I have." They walked to the outer area, where patrons relaxed on leather benches, drinking wine and cocktails. "Looks pretty unoccupied," he said, noticing there was no line to the women's bathroom, that in and of itself a small miracle. "I'll wait for you here."

Gemma looked skeptical, but she made the walk down the short corridor anyway.

What came next, Adonis would never be able to fully describe to another person. It was the oddest sound. As if all the random nonsense babble one usually heard in a crowd coalesced into two hushed words: *Gemma Hart*.

"Was that Gemma Hart?" one woman whispered to her companion.

"That's Gemma Hart," a man said to his companion.

"Didn't you work on a Gemma Hart movie? What was she like?" Two men leaned closer together.

"Is that Gemma Hart?"

The questions and comments continued. Just below hearing level, but not silent. When Gemma emerged from the bathroom, most people, but not all, had the sensitivity to change the subject. When it looked like someone was thinking of approaching her, Adonis shouldered his way through the crowd and took Gemma by the arm.

"Ready to see the rest?"

She blinked, nodded, and took him in. For a moment, it was as if she didn't know him at all. Then her eyes cleared and she smiled. "Sure. I hope the second half is as funny."

Fortunately, the second half *was* as funny, but not humorous enough to take his mind off the people in the hallway. In some ways, it went better than he'd thought. Hundreds of autograph seekers weren't making an impenetrable circle around his date. But in a way, what had happened was a hundred percent eerier.

If Dominic Andreis had taught him one thing, it was manners. It was poor form to talk about people while they were standing right in front of you. But that's exactly what had happened. Dozens of people whispering her name, not too loud, but not too soft. They talked about her as if they were oohing and ahhing over the exhibition of something rare and rarely seen—which she was. But it was as if they forgot that she was a person as well. A living, breathing person, with all five senses intact. Who could feel their stares and hear their words.

"Did you not like it?" Gemma asked when the actors gave their last bows and left the stage.

"No, it was good." He clapped a little too loudly and did his best to smooth over the frown that had probably taken over his face. "Pretty good, actually. I was just thinking."

"Are you okay to go back and see Jesse Jacobs?"

Adonis eyed his program. "He played the boyfriend?"

"Ms. Hart, Mr. Jacobs invited you backstage," an usher said before they could stand.

"Thanks. I was just going to ask how I could visit."

"You're more than welcome. Your agent or manager is welcome to call the theater to get permission in the future."

"Of course. Last-minute plans," she said, her tone apologetic. "We'll follow you."

"And he is?" The usher eyed him suspiciously. He wondered if proffering some kind of identification would have made the woman feel more comfortable.

"Adonis Andreis. My date."

The woman turned away, whispering something into a high-tech walkie-talkie. Then she led them through a series of narrow hallways until they were standing in front of a dressing room with the actor's picture and name affixed to the door.

Whether the usher noticed, he didn't know, but the deep breath Gemma took wasn't lost on him. An other-worldly calm seemed to come over her, and then she lifted her hand to knock.

SEVENTEEN

Gemma

Jesse Jacobs grabbed her in the world's biggest bear hug.

"I can't believe I haven't seen this girl since the wrap party for *Seventh Voyage*," he bellowed into her hair.

Jesse smelled as good as he'd always smelled. Some kind of earthy cologne that he'd had custom blended or something, if she remembered right. Her heart squeezed with longing the moment he let her go.

"This is my friend Adonis."

"That your real name?"

A genuine laugh escaped Gemma before she could cover her mouth or swallow it down. "It was the first question I asked him, too."

"The name fits. That's for sure." Jesse eyed her tall blond companion with appreciation. Adonis was his type. But then again, Adonis was probably every living, breathing person's type.

She could feel the heat surrounding her as she flushed

with embarrassment. She walked over to a stand of drinks and grabbed a Pellegrino before anyone could see the red blotches steal up her face. Red-faced redhead was not a good look.

"You're completely bald now?" she said as she sipped at the fizzy water.

"Yeah. Well. It's the hot look. It's either that or start putting that noxious stuff on my head, hoping more hair will grow."

Playfully, she swiped at his light brown skull liberated of its hair. "You're still one of the hottest actors in the business."

"Aw shucks, lady. You want to rent a billboard? Or even better, get my IMDb age adjusted downward."

"I think you've already shaved off five years."

"Shhh." Jesse's mock admonition was only half in jest.

"At least you're not the youngest Academy Award winner ever."

She'd started acting as a child. There were probably thousands of articles talking about her youthful Oscar win.

Jesse's lips pursed in a semi-frown. "You're thinking about it, aren't you?"

"Oscar versus five years of youth. Might be an even trade."

They both laughed a good long time. Hollywood was so crazy. But being here with Jesse reminded her why she both loved and hated the business.

"You did a great job tonight. I always loved watching you work. You're so in the moment. I wish I could disappear as easily into a role as you seem to."

"Oh, God, we can't have that hiding-your-light-under-a-bushel talk. You have an entire shelf of shiny awards."

"I know you've probably had a long night and longer week. But I'd love to have you and the guy or girl you're seeing over for dinner as soon as my house is done." She looked back at Adonis. "Maybe a few weeks from now."

"Renovations." Jesse's tone was sympathetic.

"Renovations." She threw up her hands. "It's coming in early and under budget, though."

"Good contractor?"

The weight of a thousand clichés descended on her shoulders. How many actresses had gone on to date their builders? One…a hundred. Unable to stop the heat this time, she lifted her hand toward Adonis.

"AA Construction. He's my builder."

"At least she knows you're going to show up in the morning," Jesse said, tongue firmly planted in cheek.

"I should box your ears," Gemma admonished.

"I love how you've kept all your Britishisms even though you've been here more than half your life. Speaking of which, how's your aunt Sharon. You guys square?"

"Not really. We went our separate ways after *Voyage*. I harbor no ill will." Gemma looked at her watch, hoping he didn't probe that obvious lie. "It's late. I have a super long drive and you have to get up and do this tomorrow. So great seeing you. Give me your number."

What would have usually been an exchange of information went one way, with Gemma getting Jesse's e-mail and cell number. They did the air kiss and hug, though it felt more real than most.

Jesse stuck out his right hand and Adonis took it in a firm grip, placing his other hand over their joined ones. "Nice meeting you, man. Hope to see you again."

Even though she'd have liked to stay and shoot the breeze a bit longer, she didn't want to linger too long. Wear out the welcome of an old acquaintance.

The lobby and parking lot were blissfully empty when they wound their way from the back of the theater to outside.

"Hope it was okay for you."

"Which part, Gemma?"

"All of it. The play. Jesse."

"It's all perfectly fine. There's no reason it shouldn't be."

"I kind of dragged you along," she said, clicking the unlock button on the fob. "I don't know what you do for fun."

"Do you want me to drive?" Adonis asked. "It's a long way back."

"I'm going to have to say no, okay? Sorry."

"You don't have to apologize, Gemma," he said, opening her door and helping her in before he opened the passenger door and got into the seat next to hers.

"You're right. It's not about your accident or anything."

"I didn't think it was." Though the way he said it made her think he wasn't telling the entire truth.

Gemma had to focus on clearing her mind when she navigated from the Santa Monica Freeway to the Pacific Coast Highway.

"I like to drive because it's one place in my life I can

exercise some control, yeah. When I was a kid, there was always a driver or my aunt. And even when I was older, being number two on the call sheet meant that a driver came with it. This is the first time I've picked out my own car and driven it where I want to go."

No small birds, animals, or people died on their way back to Malibu, so she marked it as a successful trip.

After the gate closed behind her, the butterflies took up flight in her stomach. Didn't a date end with shagging if both parties were willing? She was more than willing. After Jesse's comment about waking up where he worked, she imagined Adonis was ready to put some space and time between them.

She turned to him in the cab of the car. The cabin lights glowed gold on his face. She wondered if he knew how good looking he was. Ninety percent of the actors she'd worked with hadn't been half as good looking—not without a few hours of work from the best makeup artists in the business.

"You don't have a partner, do you?" she asked, instead of "do you like me" or "would you like to stay the night." Her actor's face kept her from visibly wincing.

Adonis unbuckled his seat belt and turned to her. He pried her cold hands from the steering wheel and wrapped his warm hands around them.

"Gemma—"

As soon as he started speaking, the lights of the Mercedes snapped off. She'd always wondered how long they stayed on after she went in the house. Now she knew. Not quite long enough.

Adonis didn't seem to notice the light. As soon as her

eyes adjusted, the cabin wasn't as dark as she thought it would be. There was enough light from the moon shining through the smoked-glass roof and ambient light from her outdoor security lights to see him clearly.

"Yeah?"

"I wouldn't have kissed you if I'd been committed to anyone else."

Gemma unclenched her gut with relief.

"Do you want to come inside for a drink…of water or juice? Not alcohol. I'm sorry to have pushed the sherry on you."

"You couldn't have known. I take all offers with the spirit they are given."

"Sorry…so…"

"Gemma. Stop. Stop being sorry. You do not have to apologize for having wants and desires. Just because you're rich and famous, you do not have to be sorry for wanting a human connection. It's what we all want."

"Does that mean you'll come in and have a bit of how's your father? If you're not completely shagged of course."

He dropped her hands and threw his head back in a laugh. "None of that was in English. But if it involves you and a comfortable bed, then I'm in."

Gemma hopped out of the car and punched a code into the front door. Anticipation made her hands slippery on the knob.

Granger was on the other side of the door, nose pushing through the crack as soon as it was revealed.

The dog. She'd forgotten about Granger. She'd never forgotten the dog before. Is this what sex did to people, make them forget what was important?

"I have to let Granger out," she said to Adonis.

"I'll wait in the bedroom," he said. He stepped through the door. She could hear the sound of his boots fading as he made his way up the stairs.

Gemma dropped the lead three times before she properly fitted it around the dog's neck. When she bypassed the car, she could sense the dog's agitation in his unsure gait.

"We're going to take a quick neighborhood walk. No car or beach today."

Grabbing the controller from its seat next to the garage, she pushed a button, sliding her gate open, then closed it when she and the dog were on the other side.

In the dark, she looked right, then left. She'd never walked here. The dog usually relieved himself on the property or at the beach. This area outside her gated property was a mystery. The landscape in daylight wandered through her mind. She turned left.

One of the reasons she'd bought the house was its location on a dead-end street. Once he adjusted to the strangeness of the situation, Granger snuffled along, happily sniffing and marking every spot he could find. The end of the road was a short half-mile away. When the pavement ended, she turned. By the time she was back at her gate, Granger had taken care of his needs.

Back through the gate and front door, she clicked the lead off. She plucked a bone from a basket by the door. Satisfied, Granger trotted away to a pillow tucked in a corner.

Now, her needs.

As she walked upstairs, she acknowledged that she *did*

have needs. She needed love and desire and touch. There was a beautiful man at the top of the stairs who could provide if not all, at least two.

The world would not tilt off its axis if she accepted what he was offering.

When she pushed through the door, the scent of shower gel and the humidity of the shower were the first things she noticed.

Adonis was resting on her bed, propped up on her pillows, flipping through a month-old issue of *Vanity Fair*.

"Do you have them flown in?"

"What?" she asked. Was he talking about shower soap?

"Magazines?"

"Oh, no. Not exactly. I bring them back on flights. I was in London for a weekend a couple of months back."

Avoiding the orange leather chair, instead she chose to sit on the platform. Leaning down, she picked at the tiny strap and buckle on her suede platform shoes.

Frustrated air puffed from her lips.

"Let me," Adonis said, tossing the magazine carelessly onto the floor.

A man who lifted drywall and lumber, stone and hammers, knelt before her and, with finesse she wouldn't have guessed at, unbuckled first one shoe, then the next. He shoved them under one of her chairs with a deft movement then was back.

Wordlessly, he massaged first her arches then ankles. The sheer pleasure was so decadent, she did all she could not to preen like a cat before him. Closing her eyes, she fell back against the silky duvet, letting the warmth from his hands steal up her body.

"I've been thinking of taking this dress off for hours," he whispered in her ear.

His needs and desires were a lot to process. She was used to people worshipping her, admiring her, making all sorts of indecent proposals, but none of those offers had ever come from someone who'd actually met her in person —knew her.

Her skin pricked as Adonis' hands brushed along her front and sides.

"Is there a zipper?"

Gemma lifted her right arm and hunted for the rice-grain-sized tab. Finding it, she pulled and the slider released the plastic teeth from each other.

His hand slipped through the hole at the side, causing ice and fire to ignite in her veins. Using his other hand, he lifted her bum slightly. In seconds, the heavy fabric was liberated from her body.

"Have I ever told you that you have the sexiest underwear?"

Gemma opened her eyes, staring into those of the man looking at her. Damning the decadence of it, she let her gaze roam over Adonis. From his shaggy blond hair, to his unblinking green eyes. Tentatively, she lifted a hand and smoothed it along his jaw, brushed first his lower lip then upper with her thumb. She nearly fell on the floor when he took a nip of her exploring finger.

"You're really very tidy."

"I'm going to guess that doesn't mean what I think."

She wasn't in the mood for translation. "Is your hair curly?"

His fingers combed through his short mane. "Yes. Probably. I've seen photos of me as a little guy. My mother didn't cut it for my first four or five years."

She continued her exploration, finally bold enough to see and feel what she'd wondered about, desired for the past weeks.

"Sit," she commanded. He followed her example and perched on the small piece of wood that extended beyond her mattress. This time, she did the kneeling, running each hand along a different wing of collarbone, down his biceps, hard, tense, the veins under his skin pulsing with...what? Strength, effort, strain.

Adonis sucked in air as if there were a shortage of oxygen when she scraped her nails through the hair along his chest, over his pecs, across his tiny nipples.

"Sorry."

"No need to apologize."

"You gasped. Did that hurt?"

"No, it felt good. Really good. The line, I think, between pain and pleasure is very, very fine."

"Should I stop?"

"Please, God, don't. This is the sexiest thing I've ever seen in my life as a grown man."

What? Me? She wanted to ask. But he fingered the silky strap of her bra and she forgot to be self-conscious.

His cock strained through the black briefs. She wanted to see him, touch that part of him that brought them both so much pleasure, but she didn't know how to ask. If she had to ask. What protocol required.

So she didn't ask, or apologize or fribble about. She hooked her thumbs into the sides of his briefs, and in several awkward motions, pulled them first up, and when he lifted his bum, then off.

"That's quite hard," she heard herself say.

Adonis groaned in agreement, or frustration maybe.

Standing, she offered him a hand. He accepted and followed her lead onto the bed. He lay on his back, watching, waiting.

She knelt, hesitant. Then she straddled him and laid her head upon his chest. His erection remained insistent, throbbing against the silk between her legs. His heart beat in counterpoint.

He fitted a hand along her skull, through her hair sending pins flinging about, and then down along the bumps of her spine, but he made no move to take off her bra or knickers, push inside her.

"Do you…" She didn't know how to get from where she was to what she wanted.

"I want you to take the lead."

For a long moment, she just lay there breathing in his scent mingled with her soap. Lifting up only enough to slide along his body, she met his lips with hers. She rubbed her lips against his until he opened to her.

Their tongues mated, dueled, mimicked what would happen between them in minutes. His breath was minty, warm, and his kiss turned her on like no other kiss had. A simple kiss and she was squeezing her thighs, shamelessly rubbing against his cock, trying to relieve the pressure building. But it wasn't enough.

Reluctantly, she lifted and reared back on her knees.

This time she reached around behind her and undid the clasp of the bra. It fell to his chest. She lifted it and discarded it atop the glossy magazine that had held his interest. She pulled her knickers down, and rolled off him onto her back to shimmy them off.

One second, she was tossing them toward her bra, and in the next, Adonis was rolling over her.

"I thought you wanted me to take lead."

"I was silly. I don't have the patience for that right now. Not one iota," he whispered in her ear before bringing his mouth down on hers. This was no sipping of lips or dancing of tongues. His was a soul-deep kiss that liquefied her bones.

Her hands, when she could muster up the strength, explored his back, the corded tendons of his neck, the broad planes of his scapula, the knotted muscle of his flexing bum, which was doing a little thrusting thing, his hot erection rubbing first at her hip, and after she hitched a leg over his hip, at the warm cleft between her thighs.

It was as if nothing had happened and so much had happened. But she wanted more. She wanted him. Inside.

"Condom. Do you have one?"

"Con-dom," he said, imitating her accent. "I do so love the way you say that."

Without answering what she felt was the most compelling question of the moment, he left her lips and kissed her throat, collarbone, and then his mouth—hot, hungry, greedy—took in as much of one of her breasts as possible.

Her hips reared up, losing the most precious contact with his cock. But the lips and tongue teasing her nipple were so much better, or at least a very good substitute. His mouth left one breast and moved to the other.

While she tried to gain hold, grab purchase on some part of his body, he thwarted her efforts by slipping his free hand, the one not plumping her breast for his delight, between her legs, a single finger finding her clitoris and alternately pressing and rubbing oh so slowly.

Gemma was consumed by her arousal. She wanted so much to come, to feel relief from the twisting tension, but she held back.

Seconds, or minutes later, he pulled away only long enough to fit the Durex tight over his penis. She watched, avidly interested. Her mouth watered with the knowledge that finally she'd feel fulfilled, finally she'd get what she wanted, what both of them needed.

Deeply he kissed her, holding her head firmly in place. Not allowing her to squirm when the mating of their mouths grew intense. A knee came between her slick thighs and she gasped, ready.

Slowly, he fitted himself inside her. Inch by excruciating inch, he slipped inside. Fast was what she wanted. Fast WAS what would get them both over the edge toward fulfillment. But no matter how many times she begged with her body, grabbing his ass, hair, digging her heels into his bum, he wouldn't move faster.

Deliberately, as if following the beat of the world's slowest metronome, he thrust.

"That feels really good," she breathed into his ear.

"I know. I don't want it to end, Gemma."

"But it has to," she said, so close but so far from orgasm. It was like gazing at the stars, knowing they were there, but never getting any closer to touching them no matter how hard she reached.

"It doesn't." And it didn't. She hung on that precipice for what seemed like forever. Until his hand brushed her nipple on its way down. Until it brushed against her clitoris not one, not two, but three times. Then, and only then, did her body wind up to the point of no return.

She came long and hard. Groans, cries, and screams filled her bedroom. The squeezing of her inner walls was what probably pushed him over. A minute or two after her, he was giving voice to his own satisfaction.

"That was the best," she lifted her head to check the bedside clock, "hour of my life."

"I'm with you there," Adonis said when he came back from a quick trip to the bathroom.

As if he belonged there, he slipped under the duvet and gathered her in his arms. Willingly she went, laying her head against the beating heart she could hear inside his chest.

Gemma was overwhelmed by a feeling of something she couldn't pinpoint. There was still lingering tingling between her legs that could be possible arousal, but wasn't necessary right at this moment, though she could see that the distant pulsing would and could become an insistent thrumming later. Her head was light, the usual obligations not weighing it down, replaced with what she had to call contentment with where she was, who she was, and who she was with.

She couldn't identify the last time anything like that had ever happened. Except maybe when she was nine. It was the first time she'd ever had a sleepover, and she and her friend Fiona had shared secrets well into the night. That was the last week before she'd been scouted, before she'd gone on the whirlwind audition tour for *The Red Cradle*. Before she'd been shipped to the Sierra Nevada Mountains for six months of film production.

"I want to forgive my sister." Adonis' chest rumbled with speech. "I want my sister to forgive me. My father's right. It's time to reconcile."

"People say the power of forgiveness is amazing."

"That play from tonight made me think about it. All that arguing and such made for a good play, but it doesn't really make for a good family gathering in real life."

"I could imagine."

"Can I ask you how you did it?"

"Did what?"

"Forgive your aunt."

"What?"

"When we were in the dressing room. You said to Jesse that you and your aunt were square."

Gemma disentangled from him. "I'll be right back," she said. She pulled her robe from its place on the bathroom door and took herself down the hall. Getting out a glass, she poured herself a generous measure of sherry. After gulping that down, she brought a more modest glass back to the bedroom and deposited it on the bedside table.

She gathered throw pillows that had fallen to the floor in their haste to use the bed for something other than sleeping. Only after she'd gotten back in bed and gotten comfortable did she speak.

"I'm drinking this because I honestly need it right now."

"Gemma. I'm not the alcohol police. I gave up drinking because it fucked up my life, not yours."

With that permission, she took another fortifying sip. "I'm square with my aunt because we settled the lawsuit. No reason other than that."

"Lawsuit?"

"I guess you don't watch much television."

"No offense, but watching reports of the sordid details of other people's lives isn't my thing. Not that I'm saying your life is sordid," he backpedaled.

"Maybe it is. Look, after *The Red Cradle*, I was immediately cast in another movie. *Emperor*."

"The one shot in China?"

"It was one of the first movies the Communist Party permitted. My dad's a teacher. My mum's life is really busy. By that time she couldn't just quit and spend six months in China. Enter Sharon."

"She had time?"

"She was an actress living in Venice. My mum thought she'd be a great chaperone, companion. She'd get ten percent of my earnings and she could still pursue her own career. I'd get loving supervision from a family member, not some American stranger."

"Doesn't sound like the world's worst idea."

"It probably wasn't. But it ended in a lawsuit and a restraining order."

"Didn't end good?"

"I don't know if any relationship in Hollywood does. Do you know what a Coogan account is?"

"Nope."

"Long story short, California law requires that fifteen percent of a child's pay be put in a blocked trust account."

"Fifteen?" He screwed up his eyes and shook his head in disbelief.

"I shouldn't say California. It's the same in New York. Should be eighty-five. Anyway, the kid can't get access to the account until they're of legal age. An adult needs to be put in charge of the account. That person was my aunt Sharon."

Adonis shifted so his head was against the headboard. He lifted his muscled arms and made a cradle of his hands for his head. Despite all the movement, he never broke eye contact.

"Long story short, I went to the SAG-AFTRA credit union two days after my eighteenth birthday."

"Why did you wait so long?"

"I was legless for a couple of days."

"Legless?"

"Squiffy. Drunk. Eighteen is the legal drinking age in London and I was out painting the city red. Everything was paid for, I didn't have any suspicions, really. I went because my mum mentioned that it was time that I learn how to control my own finances."

"Then what?"

"The what was that there was maybe half the money I'd been expecting. Took me weeks of pouring over old bank statements with my dad, but we figured Sharon started off depositing the ninety percent she and my parents had agreed upon. But as my career got bigger and her work dried up, I think. I guess. I don't know. I think she got jealous. I mean I was stupid. All the signs were there. She rented out her bungalow in Venice and moved us into a big house in Los Feliz. Designer purses and shoes came in the door nearly every day. But I didn't want to be suspicious, I think. I chalked it up to the free stuff celebrities get and just got on one plane or another to film the next movie."

"But you had to sue?"

"Never sue when you're angry," Gemma started. "That's what the lawyers said to me. But I was hurt by her betrayal with Andy O'Bryan."

"Geez. Him again?"

"When I hired the forensic accountant, Sharon got mad. She visited me on set. Shut down production while she screamed that she'd given everything up for me and I owed her. She said her youth was gone. Her opportunities were gone. I owed her for taking that away, making her miss the prime acting time of her life babysitting me."

"What does that have to do with O'Bryan?"

"Andy's good, but not that clever. Sharon was in on the tape with him. She dolled me up and got me to go over there. She's the one with the foreign connections who got them money for the video."

"Two people who were supposed to love you…"

"Sold me to the highest bidder," she said completing the sentence he'd left hanging. Gemma downed the remaining liquid. It burned a path past the lump in her throat. She swallowed hard. Betrayal was a bitter pill.

Breath puffed from Adonis' lips. "Jesus, aren't we a pair."

"Don't go by me. Your relationship with Zoe sounds reparable. It was a really terrible thing that happened.

You two can probably, if not put it behind you, then maybe put family first and make the best of it going forward."

"You, Gemma Hart, are very wise." His yawn was wide and unapologetic. He turned over, pulling the duvet over his shoulder. Already looking half asleep, he said, "I have to get to sleep so I'm not late for work in the morning."

She almost protested, but then he made a broad wink and closed both his eyes.

EIGHTEEN

Adonis

"Come with me tonight," he said to Gemma, doing the cryptic thing she always did. He looked down at her from the ladder. He didn't have a hammer to drop. The dog sat at her side, looking as perplexed as she about getting an invitation for a date from the top of a ladder.

"Where?" Gemma looked around, unconsciously gripping the dog's collar, like he was going to secret them all away to the Bermuda Triangle or a castle dungeon.

"My dad's having one of his family dinners. In the last ten years, I've never shown up. Not once. Today, I'm hungry." He inserted the metal can for the last recessed lighting fixture and came down off the ladder. He took a good look around the large open-plan area. It was almost done, and would look great in his portfolio. The custom farmhouse cabinets would go well with the furniture his father had described in her storage unit.

"Does he cook?" she asked when they were once again on the same level.

"Great Greek food. He makes decent Italian as well, though my mother would never admit that."

"Your mum's Italian?"

"Was. She died when I was still a kid."

"I'm sorry."

"For once, I'm not going to say anything about you apologizing."

"It was appropriate this time, right?" Her question was so sincere, he wanted to hug her. Kiss her. Tell her it was all going to be okay. That it would get easier one day. That she was well on her way to getting it right.

"Absolutely. So dinner tonight?"

"I'm not, I want you to know, completely full of myself. But I would have to be deaf, dumb, and blind to not have a certain…shall we say…awareness of how my presence can change a room. Not everyone wants to be in that room. Most of the time *I* don't want to be in that room."

"I want to be with you, the Gemma Hart that I'm getting to know. And I won't lie and say that you may disarm my sister and make my reconciliation plan just that much easier."

"Plus, your family isn't, as I recall, my biggest fan. I think your brother…Nicki, is it? I didn't make the greatest first impression."

He tried not to visibly shudder at that image, his dad collapsed on the floor, and Gemma freaking out about calling an ambulance. Nicki having to drive his dad to the only urgent care center in the town.

"They will love you," he said, because he did…like

her…a lot, that is. "I know all about bad first impressions. Fortunately, they can be reformed."

"What kind of dinner is this? Would I be crashing? I'm imagining a formal table set for eight and the ninth wheel shows up." She looked for all the world like she'd been the ninth wheel one time too many.

"Is that the British equivalent of the fifth wheel?"

"No," she laughed. That jittery but warm feeling filled his body. The one he'd come to associate with merely being in her presence. Made him feel light and young again. "I made that up."

"Never crashing. My brother's soon-to-be wife does these dinners too. I think they like to be social, cook, meet new people. From what I hear, there are always a few strays."

"I'm like a stray dog?" Gemma and Granger looked at each other. He'd have said the dog was full of mock outrage if he thought the dog could understand their conversation.

"Little bit. But we'll feed you, and give warm hugs."

She stepped forward and wrapped her arms around his waist. Laid her head on his chest. "Can I think about it?"

"I have a better idea. Say yes, and bring your friend Jesse. You said you wanted to see him again. Sounds like you guys had more to talk about."

She unwrapped her arms. Immediately he missed her, even though she was there in the room with him. It was the oddest thing he'd ever experienced.

"I'll call him," she said.

It was a good few seconds after she and the dog left

the room that he remembered what they were talking about.

Ten minutes later, she was back, phone in hand. "He's in. But he needs to know the where and when."

"Seven thirty." He pulled a small pad and pen from his back pocket. Flipping past the measurements for office shelves he'd yet to install, he scratched out Dominic's address on the small lined pad and tore the paper from it.

"Are we...do you want to drive together?" Her question was the usual combination of confidence and hesitance that were the two sides of the same person.

"I have to get home first. It depends on traffic. I can call you. Or I can't because I don't have your phone number."

"Right." She shifted in her flip-flops, uncomfortable as hell. He didn't feel the least bit guilty about it.

"We've gone out on dates, Gemma, had sex. I've slept in your house. All without shouting it to the rooftops or selling you out to tabloids."

Her brow furrowed as she worked through questions of trust. Gemma let out a deep sigh.

"Three-one-zero," she started. He pulled his phone from the other free pocket and typed as fast as he could. Something told him she wasn't likely to repeat the number.

"It's covered by the NDA."

That statement relaxed her. Her shoulders came down from around her ears. "Right. Casual. I'll have to go see what I can find to wear."

"That dress from the other night was really great."

"That's because you got to take it off me. There's no

mystery there. I'll find something else that's a bit easier to get off."

The thought of removing her dress kept him going the next few hours, through a needed meeting, and helped him resist the urge to bail like he'd done whenever he'd promised to get together with the family.

Later, thoughts of rejection and awkward silences—or worse, yelling and recriminations—pushed sex and easy-on, easy-off clothes from his mind. He circled the block a couple of times, not seeing her car, but seeing a long line of parked cars in front of his dad's house. Lights blazed from Dominic's bottom unit.

He made his next circle wider, hoping the swift moving traffic on Beverly would distract him from the potentially awkward scene what awaited him.

A text lit up his phone. *I'm parked on the corner of Orange and Oakwood.*

Gemma was here.

He wanted his family to meet her, realize she wasn't the self-centered monster they'd made her out to be.

A little voice in his head suggested he'd invited her so he couldn't back out, run away. Not this time.

When he came to a complete stop at a light, he responded. *I'll find you in about ten minutes.*

The Mercedes that looked shiny and flashy in the driveway of her house was fairly nondescript on a street full of other such luxury vehicles. He knocked on the darkly-tinted window. It eased down in a smooth mechanical motion.

"Ready?" he asked of the red-haired beauty that appeared.

"As I'll ever be."

The window eased back up with a nearly silent whirr. He heard the sound of the locks pop, and pulled at the door handle. Gemma offered him her hand and he took it, helping her step down from the SUV.

"You look amazing," he said. It wasn't a lie. Her auburn hair shone under the streetlamp. The dress she was wearing was a simple gray sweater thing, but it clung to her breasts. He smoothed his hand along the yarn. It was as soft as it looked.

Damned dinner.

What in the hell kind of idea had that been? He wanted to slip his hands under the turtleneck dress and ease it up until he could see what lacy underwear she had, pull it off her. His fantasies instantly had them in her roomy back seat. The dress would be hiked up around her breasts, her nipples hard and wet from his mouth. Him pushing into her until she screamed his name.

"Adonis?"

He snapped back to the present. To the most beautiful woman in the world standing by her car in a dress and heels, ready to meet his sister.

"Is Jesse here?" he asked as they stood under the streetlight.

"He's maybe ten or twenty minutes out. Lives in West Hollywood. It's hell getting out of that city no matter what the time of day."

The look she gave him. Trust. Guilelessness. He bent down and kissed the gloss off her lips. Kissed her while holding her bottom in his hand. Kissed her until someone beeped and whistled their approval.

"We should go," he said.

"Right. Yeah. Cheers." At least her blue eyes looked as unfocused and as cloudy as his brain felt.

Grabbing a big light blue purse, she checked her watch and locked the car.

"We're going to be a bit late." Her voice held worry about disrespect, disapproval from his family.

"I think the time is a suggestion," he reassured her.

Adonis grabbed her hand and tried to keep his breath even. Thoughts of seeing his sister killed his erection, thank God. But ramped up the worry about what he was planning to say, do when he walked in the door.

Suddenly it seemed like the stupidest, most ridiculous idea ever to have brought Gemma along. Except he liked her, and wanted to be with her. And he wanted his family to know her, see what he saw in his movie star lover. Prove that she was more than a recluse with a reluctance to dial nine-one-one.

When they made it to the house, up the stairs, and down the path, which seemed more like a plank extending from a pirate ship, he knocked.

A vaguely familiar guy answered. *Max*. That was his name. He'd met him at the hospital when Zoe was visiting his father. Shit. Shit. Shit. He didn't think he'd made a good first impression. He'd probably acted like an asshole and insulted his sister in front of this guy. This night of so-called reconciliation wasn't off to the best start.

Max's guarded expression proved him right.

"This is Gemma," he said. "I'm Adonis, we met a few months ago," he said, trying to get out in front of the thing. He thrust out his hand in greeting.

"I remember." Max took his hand in a firm, not quite punishing, grip.

For once, memory wasn't a good thing.

Gemma extended her hand, quite innocently. Max's eyes shot to her left forearm, the one holding the huge bag, then widened.

"Is that a Rolex?"

"What? This?" She peered at the silver- and blue-faced watch on her left wrist. "It is. I like the blue face." She held up her arm higher. "Matched the purse."

"Do you like watches?" Max asked. A half-smile covered his face. Much more welcoming than the stormy look he'd given Adonis.

Gemma glanced back at Adonis as if to ask, "Should I like watches?" He racked his brain for the world's longest second then remembered that Max had some kind of jewelry store side business or something. He tried to make his nod as imperceptible as possible.

"They're nice. I have a few. This one was a gift from my agent last Christmas."

"You have a nice agent," Max said appreciatively. "That's a Lady-Date just twenty-eight. That'll age pretty well. Be worth a mint years from now."

"Do you want a car?" Gemma asked.

She'd passed the first test, but this one was a flunker. Cars were not host gifts.

"What?" Max asked, his face a mask of confusion.

"This year I got a car for my birthday. Some super-hard-to-get plug-in SUV thing with doors that open like wings. I like the watch better than the car."

"Why don't you come in," Max said, the moment

having gone from congenial to awkward. "Maybe someone here could use a hybrid."

"A hybrid what?" Dominic asked, coming to the door. His dad had a gold chain hanging on his wrist next to a dish towel. Was this night going to be about expensive jewelry? He tried to remember the last time he'd seen his father in anything other than his wedding ring.

"Hello, Dad." He tried for lighthearted, congenial. Didn't quite make it. "Decided to take you up on the invitation for once."

"Well aren't you a sight for sore eyes." His dad's eyes did shine a bit brighter than usual. "And you brought a lady friend. Well now, this is going to be interesting. Good to see you, Gemma," he said, pulling her in for a big hug. She went awkwardly into his embrace.

The winking gold Adonis expected to reflect the recessed lighting was gone. His father didn't have his wedding ring on.

He dismissed the thought almost as quickly as it had come. Probably took it off for some kind of work project. He was getting distracted by anything that would take his mind off what he was really there to do—make things right with his sister.

"Thanks for letting me crash, Mr. Andreis." Gemma was the model of British politeness.

"You stood over my lifeless body. I think that puts us on a first-name basis. Call me Dominic."

"I brought this for you, Dominic," Gemma said. From her bag, she produced a small ribbon-wrapped box.

His dad took the box, sniffed at it. Adonis tried his best to see what it was. When his dad brought it down from his nose, he squinted at it. Looked like a box of small mackerel.

"These don't stink like fish."

"They're hand-painted sardines from Rococo. It's a chocolatier in London that makes them. I always buy them, but can never eat them."

"But you think I'd have no problem biting the head off a fish."

Adonis knew Dominic was joshing, but didn't know if Gemma got his father's old school sense of humor. From what he knew of British humor, it was a lot of *Benny Hill* and word play too clever for him.

"You seem like the head-biting type," she said. Her delivery was totally deadpan.

His father practically fell down laughing. She'd nailed it.

"C'mon in. Speaking of fish, I have some real sardines for dinner tonight. You eat fish?"

"Grew up on them. Mostly wrapped in newspaper from the chip shop, but I'm willing to give yours a go."

Dominic threw the door wide in welcome. The room was warm. His sister was standing behind the couch, her hand on Max's shoulder. Holly and Nicki were there, but he didn't see his little niece. Maybe they'd found a babysitter for the night.

"Forty thousand dollars?" Zoe's question could be heard above everyone else. He'd never describe his sister as quiet or shy or retiring. Her question, coupled with Gemma's entrance, silenced the room.

It was exactly the opposite of what he'd expected. His

family, his Midwestern, down-to-earth brother and sister, were acting like star struck teens.

Holly, his brother's fiancée, was the first to speak after the world's longest and most awkward pause. "You're Gemma Hart! Welcome. I'm Holly Prentice. I think you've already met almost everyone else here. Zoe, please introduce yourself."

Gemma threw him a look. For once, he could read her mind. Nope, she didn't need ID. Probably never would.

With a civility he didn't think he could ever muster, Gemma shook everyone's hands, even Zoe's. The two new arrivals stood shifting their weight for a few seconds before they were saved by the doorbell.

Dominic, suddenly animated again, pulled open the door.

"Howdy do," he said. "Dominic Andreis."

Gemma looked around and practically ran toward the door like a lifeline was on the other side.

"Jesse, glad you could come," she said as her friend crossed the threshold. He thrust a bottle of wine at Dominic then took Gemma in a hug. "I brought my friend Alex Marroquin."

Jesse stepped aside and a man stepped forward. "I'm Alex. Nice to meet all of you. Hey, Nick, is that you?" Alex stepped toward the couch and Nick rose. The two men embraced like long-lost friends.

"Alex did some voice-over work for me on the Esperanza Nueva documentary," Nick said to no one in particular.

The tension broke then. "Let me show you the place,"

Adonis said. "You don't mind, Dad?" he asked as almost an afterthought.

"No, you should impress your lady with your fine carpentry skills," his father said with a wink.

Before either one of them could protest the characterization, Dominic had disappeared into the kitchen.

He'd save that room for last. Instead, he showed Gemma the work he and his dad had done on the nearly hundred-year-old two-family house. They were in the bedroom when she looked him in the eye.

"So it's a semi-detached?"

Adonis laughed. "I have no idea what you're talking about. But maybe we can talk about it later when I'm in the mood for translation. I'm really glad that you came," he said, then bent to kiss her. There was something so right about this. Him, her, here with his family. Gemma rose to her tiptoes and wrapped her arms around his neck.

It was so good. It was too good. Gently, he lifted his mouth from hers, unwound her arms. He used his thumb to wipe away the gloss that had gone where no lip stuff should go. She looked insanely hot, but not at-your-parents'-house appropriate, with her well-kissed mouth and flushed cheeks. Something had to give.

"Your house will be done in a week," he said. He grabbed her pinkie with his and pulled her back into the living room, where the smell of olive oil, lamb, and garlic was strong.

"Painting next?"

He nodded. "Then some final touches. You have movers set up?"

"Sylvester will arrange it. I can't wait to have my stuff back. To be able to use my whole house again."

The last few weeks, they'd existed in some kind of bubble. Where nothing from the outside came in. Where they didn't have to go outside for satisfaction. What came next was anyone's guess. But he wanted more. He wasn't ready to be excluded from Gemma's inner circle.

"You hungry?"

"Sure," she said.

His dad was carrying a meze platter that looked ten feet wide. He dropped Gemma's hand and caught one side of the platter and helped Dominic move it to the dining room. It was heaped with olives, chunks of feta, figs, and two kinds of ham, and a whole slew of other Greek goodies.

"Don't move," Dominic said after the platter was situated. He stuck his head around the open archway. "Zoe, do your thing."

The two-finger whistle that came from his sister silenced the small crowd.

"Food is on the table," his father announced to the quiet room. Dominic was not someone to cross, so everyone dutifully came into the dining room. The red velvet chairs had been pushed back from the table. The sound of plates and cutlery gathered from the sideboard were the only in the room.

Zoe's eye caught his then skittered away. His sister seemed suddenly preoccupied with touching her boyfriend's back and guiding him through eating as though the guy were a starving man at his first meal. Then she picked at her own food.

It was now or never. Except for Jesse and Alex, these were all of the people he needed to make peace with. These were all the people he loved, and who hopefully still loved him.

"Zoe," he said, making sure his voice was heard. "I think it's time we talk."

His sister's dark Greek skin paled more than he thought was possible. Her green eyes, so much like his, so much like Nicki's, rounded with shock. She dropped her plate to the table and brandished her knife and fork as if to ward him off like an evil spirit.

He shook his head, not yielding to her.

"No, it's time."

NINETEEN

Dominic

Dominic watched his two oldest children, the two most stubborn people he'd ever met in his life, stand across his dining room and stare at each other. Either his greatest dream was about to come true or he was about to watch the world's biggest disaster. Truth was, it could go either way, and there was nothing he could do to influence the outcome.

He wanted to intervene, wanted to pray to God to keep his family together, pray that his late wife could wield some kind of magical powers down from heaven to fix his two broken children. Instead, he figuratively sat on his hands.

"You used to be my best friend," his first-born started, oblivious to the wide-eyed, open-mouthed stares of everyone in the room. "It was the two of us against the world," Adonis continued. "Especially after we lost Mom. I have a lot of regrets in life. A lot. But my biggest regret is losing you."

"We don't have to do this, Adonis. Isn't it enough that we can be in the same room without arguing? That's progress enough."

"No, it's not enough, Zoe. I'm not living a full life. Over the last month, I've seen what it's like to live a limited life. It's not the way I want to live out my years. I don't want to turn forty with any of this unresolved."

Dominic looked at Gemma, his son obviously referencing her. She didn't get the reference, or she cared too much about his son to let it bother her. Either way it was a point in her favor.

"What about Emily?" Zoe asked. She tried to keep her stare hard, her voice sharp. But Dominic could see and hear the cracks. A dozen years later and his daughter was still in pain.

Dominic cursed himself a thousand times for not fixing this earlier. Fixing this when it would have been easier. But he'd let Zoe think her brother was an asshole. He'd been in that hospital emergency room holding her hand as she'd slipped in and out. Listened with her as the doctor told her she'd been drugged with something called ketamine.

When the doctor had mentioned that one of the side effects was memory loss, he'd been grateful. Grateful that his daughter could go on to lead a normal life free of the memory of almost being assaulted. All these years he thought he'd protected her by letting her live with a half-truth.

Standing there with two parts of his heart standing outside of his chest, he knew he'd made a mistake—one that had hurt both his children.

"I'm sorrier than you could ever imagine. So very sorry. But there's nothing I can do. Nothing in this whole world that can change what happened or bring Emily back. If I could trade my life for hers, don't you think I'd do it?"

The pain of that hit Dominic sharp under the breastbone.

"But it doesn't work that way," Adonis said. "I'm here. You're here. We should love each other because we're all that we have left."

"You should tell her all of it," Gemma Hart whispered into the strained silence.

"She's right," Dominic said. He shouldn't have spoken, but he couldn't help himself.

"What? Everything? I was there, Adonis." His daughter's voice went hoarse. "I was right there the whole time. You did that fucking macho big brother thing that I hated and insisted that you drive. I was supposed to do the driving. I would never have drank and driven."

"It wasn't my plan, Zoe. Even without the accident, I knew how stupid that was."

"So why did you do it?"

"They roofied you."

Dominic could see years of his daughter believing one thing disrupted by something completely different.

"I took your advice and decided to have a drink with those college guys. And it was fun. We shot tequila, talked about girls and cars. I was twenty-five and didn't have a lot of guy friends. It was like borrowing a frat for the night. But a few drinks in, I realized you'd disappeared. I may have been buzzed, Zoe, but I still took my responsibility as your big brother very seriously. Very. And I hadn't seen you for an hour, even more, maybe. The thing about guys is they act really stupid in groups. Really, really stupid."

"I remember from high school." Her voice had softened into something approaching forgiveness.

"I'm not saying this to blame you, but you and Emily had shown up half naked. And the more the guys talked, the more I realized they had ideas about that. There were only like four or five of you girls there. And about twenty guys. I went upstairs to find the two of you. You and Emily were lying in bed not acting like yourselves."

"So he got you out," Gemma chimed in.

Dominic hadn't been expecting that. His son and the actress were much closer than he'd thought. He'd have to file that one away to think about later. Much later.

"He talked to you about this?" Zoe rounded on Gemma.

"He's been living with guilt about making two wrong decisions that night, not just one."

"Jesus." His daughter, the stoic one who never let on she was hurt, looked crushed. "I need..." She didn't finish her thought. Instead, she disappeared into the back of the house.

He looked at his oldest son. Slapped him upside the head. "Go talk to your sister. Go make up. Let me die a happy man."

He would have never thought her capable, but Gemma, with Jesse's help, pulled out the stops. That's why they were called entertainers. The two of them told bawdy backstage stories that broke the tension. They were passing out food like hosts, all the while keeping everyone laughing, distracted from the sometimes raised voices coming from the back of the apartment.

Unable to resist the call of his kids, he wandered back to his room. In time to see his first-born son and his only daughter hugging like they used to when they were a united front against him and Iris. He never thought he'd miss being ganged up on, but if that united front replaced this rift, this chasm that had been as wide as the Grand Canyon, he'd be happy to be the odd man out.

The minute his kids came back into the room, he ran to the kitchen to get the main dish of the night, moussaka, from the warming drawer.

"You haven't eaten much," Dominic said to Gemma. "You hungry?"

"I don't eat much," she said, eyeing the food like a starving man at a buffet.

"I'll cut you a little portion."

"Thanks," she said graciously.

She was thin. Thinner than most people. He wanted to feed her as much as he wanted to honor her need to stay employable. It was a hell of a struggle. He went to the kitchen to bring in some dirty dishes, to avoid being a food pusher. Kept himself busy in there for a good ten minutes to hide the tears of joy leaking down his chin. Things were going to get better with his kids. He could just sense it. The thought brought a smile to his face. He had good news as well.

As if on cue, the front doorbell rang, and he ran to answer it before anyone else did.

"Bridget," he said, kissing her on both cheeks. "Ryan."

He shook the hand of her youngest son. "Thanks for carrying her over. Do you want dinner? There's plenty."

Ryan lifted his nose and sniffed like he was a starving hound. Did no one in Los Angeles eat? He made general introductions and got two more dinner plates.

When everyone who'd wanted them had seconds, he gathered the plates and loaded the dishwasher.

He brought out strong Greek coffee, as well as walnut-stuffed figs and cranberry-stuffed phyllo. He hadn't cooked this much in years, but he'd been feeling very domestic lately, especially with all his kids within spitting distance.

He lifted his ouzo glass and hit it with a fork. The universal gesture for quiet got the desired result.

"I have an announcement to make." He gestured to his girlfriend. "Bridget, please come up here." Once Bridget joined him, he looked out on the crowd of friends, old and new. "I've asked Bridget Becker to become my wife. She's said yes. We're planning to get married before the end of the year. We hope you'll join us."

He waited a beat. Two. No one said anything.

Then the room filled with hugs, kisses, and congratulations. There wasn't a naysayer in the bunch.

"I told you." He turned to Bridget. "We raised these kids right."

TWENTY

Gemma

"Adonis is done with the house." It came out just as she'd practiced. Smooth. Clear. No stuttering. No crying.

"Isn't it great to get your house back? Renovations have to be the very definition of delayed gratification."

"Very true. It's a test of endurance."

"Are you happy with the way things turned out?" Giovanni asked, as though they were discussing counter-tops and backsplashes and not her heart being wrenched in two. The bubble where she and Adonis had spent the last weeks, him working, her talking, them making love nearly every night, was bursting. And she had no idea what in the hell she was going to do next.

She played along. "It's nice. I got my wine from storage. All the furniture is in place. Everything is clean as a whistle. He had a service that got all the dust out."

"Even I didn't have that. I swear years later, I still find the occasional thing in the back of the closet with a swath of white dust in a crease somewhere."

"Right. So…"

"What?"

"I thought things would change when my house was perfect." As if hammers had a thing to do with people. She thought there'd be friends, and gatherings, and some kind of change.

"And did they?"

"Well, my house is perfect. I mean *Vanity Fair*, *House and Garden* worthy." Nothing else had changed. Except for adding a likely temporary Adonis to the mix, it was the same as before. Her, Sylvester, and Granger. An unlikely trio versus the world.

"Do you want to be featured in one of those? I'm sure your people could arrange it."

"Maybe," she said, continuing the inane conversation out loud, while ignoring the one in her head. "Maybe people wouldn't see me as crazy if they could see that I had a normal house with bathrooms and a refrigerator."

"Or you could talk to people."

"I talk to Adonis. I met his family. I even talked to Jesse and some of his friends the other night."

"How was it?"

"I drove to West Hollywood. He made dessert at his house. Hummingbird cake and peanut butter pie. Total Americana."

"And?"

"It was fun. You know how drama is crack cocaine for actors. Thankfully it was a drug-free night." They'd treated her as normal. They had their own television shows, movies, and agents to worry over.

"Will you do it again?"

"Maybe. I'm glad I hooked up with Jesse. I didn't realize how much I missed my friends."

"You called them friends."

"Maybe not quite friends. But they could have been if I'd kept in touch. Answered e-mails and stuff instead of filtering everything through Sylvester."

"How did Sylvester end up being your only confidant?" It was the question she knew had been on Giovanni's mind. She could tell Adonis wondered too.

"I know Sylvester's a tosser. But he's direct and he's honest. Two traits that you and I know are missing in L.A. He was the only person who could keep the crazy at bay. He stopped my aunt from spending my money and sending me out for jobs that weren't right for me. He got Andy to apologize and pull most of the tapes. I know he's abrasive and not that nice, but he stuck up for me when no one else would."

"And now. Now that you're meeting people and making friends?"

"Loyalty is worth something." It was actually worth everything. But she was done explaining Sylvester to anyone. She'd probably keep him on her payroll until one of them kicked the bucket. This wasn't about Sylvester, though. She had a much bigger thing she had to contend with. It was so hard being alone. It was so hard admitting she knew nothing of life, friends, men.

Sucking in a deep breath, she did what she'd come for. "Can I ask you a question though?"

"Go ahead."

"How do you know if you're in love or if it's just physical?"

Giovanni's head snapped around like she'd announced she'd taken up stripping part time. His eyebrows kissed his hairline. He couldn't have looked more shocked. She was so glad she hadn't brought up her and Adonis' relationship at Jesse's party like she'd wanted to. So proud she hadn't brought the crack to the party. Giovanni was enough.

"Do you think you're in love?"

She examined every one of the six words in his question. Did he think she didn't know her own mind and heart? Did he think she was too inexperienced to know better? The question had been a dress rehearsal for Adonis, and so far not so good.

"I don't know. Maybe." Her tone carefully crafted, offhand. She might be in therapy, but she would never reveal what it had taken to make that almost admission.

"With Adonis?"

Who else, her heart cried out. "It's not like I have a line of suitors knocking down my door," she said with a small laugh.

"You could, Gemma. You could crook your little finger and have all the men in the world to choose from."

"I don't want all of them. None of the three and a half billion. I kind of want one."

"Have you told him?"

"How's that conversation going to go? 'Hi, thanks for the hookup. You want to turn it into something serious?'"

"Yes, Gemma. Exactly like that."

"Oh."

She practiced and rehearsed all the way home. But she wasn't a screenwriter. She didn't have a John Williams score. When she opened the door and let herself in, it was with the knowledge that she had nothing more to offer Adonis than herself. She was afraid that wasn't enough.

♥

ADONIS WAS on the floor with an iron and some sort of rag. Puffs of steam billowed toward the ceiling.

"What are you doing?"

"Smoothing out the dent from the hammer."

Embarrassment caused heat to shoot through her body, all ending up in her face. She pressed her cool hands against her warm cheeks, remembering that first day she'd talked to him and asked him to shag her. She was thrilled with the outcome, if not the way it had come about.

"Right. Sorry." She watched steam rise from the floor. Then he lifted the cloth and the iron from the wood, and it was as if there had never been a dent there in the first place. He gave her a look. "Sorry for saying sorry."

"Right as rain." He stood, put the iron on the stone countertop.

"That was like magic." It really was. He was exceptionally talented at what he did. She'd gotten lucky in more ways than one.

"Heat and water caused the wood to swell, assuming its original shape." Adonis dusted off his butt before sitting on one of the gray leather stools that faced the matching countertop of her peninsula.

"That's a great little trick for the builder's toolkit." She sat on the stool next to him. There wasn't a thing left to be done on her house. They'd crossed out everything on the punch list. It was now or never. She couldn't get the words out of her mouth, though, so she swallowed and turned to face him.

"You went out without Granger," Adonis said, not quite asking the question he probably wanted the answer to. The thing that was standing in between them like some kind of phantom.

"I was seeing Giovanni," she said. She'd rarely left without the dog, but he'd been following Adonis around like a puppy, so she left the two in male solidarity and companionship. Or maybe she thought he'd feel guilty leaving the dog alone, so he'd stay.

"You say you don't have many friends, but you two seem close."

"He's my psychologist, Adonis," she admitted.

Light brown eyebrows rose up to dark blond hair. She was all shock and awe today. "I didn't mean to pry, I had no idea."

Why was everything she said so surprising? Didn't he get it? She thought he got it. That she was human, normal. Well, maybe not normal, but subject to the same human frailties as everyone else.

"It's not something I'm ashamed of. It's just something I keep private." Because privacy was all she had. All that was left. Everyone else in the world had access to the rest, her body, her image.

"Why?"

"I'm not crazy," she prefaced. "I decided in June that I needed help. I needed to change something about my life. I was busy making my house perfect, but I wasn't fixing what was wrong on the inside."

"What's wrong?"

"Are you making fun of me?" He knew the answer, but she explained it again anyway. "Up until September, I'd been the thirty-year-old virgin. The girl who got duped into doing a sex tape. The girl whose aunt had sold her to the highest bidder. All that. All of it was wrong."

"Never. I'd never make fun of you. I'm sorry that things have been so hard. I'm sure to most people it looks like you've won the lottery."

"You're not the first person to say that. But people telling me how lucky I was, how fortunate I was, didn't help. I was angry at being violated. I needed to do something with all the anger I have...or had. My boyfriend and aunt colluded to do what they did to me. Somewhere along the way, I'd stopped being in control of my life. People like Elton Lamb and Sylvester were making decisions for me. I needed help deciding if I was ever going to act again. Or what to do instead."

"I hear you."

"I love my parents, I really do. But I needed someone from this life I've made here to help me figure out how to live, given who I am. Who I've become."

"I'm glad you have someone to talk to," he said, as though there was going to be one less person to talk to when he turned his van around and drove it from her driveway one final time.

"Today's your last day, isn't it?" she finally gathered up the courage to ask.

"I've puttered around here for a week fixing every possible nick, scratch, and dent. There's nothing left for me to do."

"There's one thing left." She stood, and he followed her upstairs.

"I didn't do any work on your bedroom," he said, looking around, confused. He was acting pretty thick for such an otherwise smart man.

She stood on tiptoe and laid a hand on either side of his jaw. Her belly twisted with love, desire, hope, need, and so much other stuff that she closed her eyes for a long moment.

Opened them again. He was there. His pupils were growing, the green of his eyes disappearing. He didn't say a word. Neither did she. She pulled his head down and brushed her lips across his. He opened and they stayed like that for how long, she couldn't say. Breathing each other's air, eyes locked in a battle of some kind, though she couldn't say what side she was on, whether she wanted to win or lose.

Her thighs shook with arousal and the effort to reach him. Rocking back on her heels, she stepped toward the bed, but didn't break her stare. She crossed her hands and lifted her cashmere turtleneck from the bottom, up and over her head. His gasp let her know he was as moved as she.

The button on her black jeans was next, then zipper. She shimmied out of them, adding the cotton to the heap on the floor. When she reached behind her back to unhook her bra, Adonis came forward and stopped her movement.

"Jesus, you have the sexiest underwear I've ever seen." He traced a hand along the top of her sky-blue lace bra cup. Swallowing, she followed the progress of his hands as they skimmed her sides then traced the outline of her thong until his fingers were pressing between her legs. "So hot. So wet. God, Gemma, I can't get enough."

She stepped back until she was leaning against the bed, just out of his reach. This time, she unhooked the bra, her breasts spilling forward. The thong was next.

She scooted back on the bed, propped herself up on her elbows, bent her knees and spread her legs. Her message couldn't have been any more blatant if she'd spoken it out loud. She was his.

Had her boldness rendered him mute?

For a long minute, he just looked. Then a slow smile spread across his mouth. That rarely seen smile made her want to touch herself, but she resisted. She didn't want to overwhelm him with this newfound courage, or maybe it was desperation. She didn't want to examine too closely.

Adonis' striptease was a near mirror of hers. First, his sweatshirt came off, then a heather-gray T. He kicked off his low-cut suede boots, then his jeans followed. He reached a hand into his briefs and pulled out his cock. Slowly, deliberately, he stroked himself from hard to steel.

She couldn't help herself. One hand drifted between her thighs, shocked at how wet she was just from looking and thinking with so little touching and tasting. Gemma spread that moisture throughout her folds, then, zeroing in on her clit, let her eyes drift to his hand, his cock.

In a moment, he was at the edge of the bed.

"You make me so fucking hard," he said. He started to move toward the bedside table. She knew he'd be looking for a condom, and she wanted him inside her, but her mouth was watering for something different. She changed position so that she was sitting on her haunches.

"Gemma—"

She didn't let him finish. She wrapped her hand around his, stilling it against his flesh, then took as much of his cock as she could into her mouth. The taste of him, that slightly salty musk, nearly sent her over the edge. For a second he put up a token protest, which was quickly replaced by grunts of approval and urgent directions on pressure and technique.

"I'm going to come, love," he said.

Pulling her mouth back, she looked up at him. "That's what I want."

"God damn, I want to be inside you. Turn over."

She got on her hands and knees.

"Jesus, your ass is amazing. You're trying to kill me today."

She didn't respond, instead waiting in anticipation for what she knew was coming. The tearing of a foil wrapper tightened the coil winding in her womb. The sound of him smoothing on the sheath. Then a warm hand stroked down her back, sliding around to tweak at her breasts, heavy with arousal.

"God damn," he said again, then he took her with one hard and swift stroke.

With no word of warning, he pounded into her again and again, so hard that her hands slid out from under her and she fell forward on her elbows. The friction from her nipples against the linen bedspread, coupled with his hand on her clit and his deep thrusting, sent her over before she had a moment to breathe, to absorb all the stimuli. A minute or two later, he broke his steady rhythm. His body jerked as he came.

Her legs gave out and she collapsed on the bed. He fell on top of her and they lay like that, as her heartbeat slowed.

"I'm sorry," he said. She felt bereft when he pulled out and disappeared into her bathroom.

She pulled back the covers and slipped under them. The room was cool now that the sun was close to setting. The marine layer was working its way in, shrouding them in gray mist. He stood by the bathroom door, nude and unselfconscious. She could barely swallow the fear that these were their last moments together.

"Do you have another job lined up?" she asked, stupidly jealous of the next woman or man who'd have Adonis in their house for eight hours a day.

"Not until January," he said, crossing his arms across his chest. "Not a lot of people like having workers in their house during the holidays."

She'd love to have this particular builder in her house during the holidays, but she didn't speak the words aloud. She wanted to say, I love you. She wanted to ask him to stay with her and Granger until New Year's. But wisdom and courage were not close companions. Holiday fantasies floated in her head. Maybe there was a way to convince him to spend at least another couple of weeks together.

"Will you come to London with me?"

"London?"

Jesse had made some calls. She had an audition with a London stage director. But she wasn't ready to reveal that, jinx the possibility of something good, so she tried to make it seem as casual as possible. "I kind of want to check in on my house there. I miss custard tarts and Cornish pasties."

"How long?"

"A couple of weeks maybe? Oh, gosh. Do you have a passport? I hear Americans don't —"

"I have a passport, Gemma. I've traveled with Dad to Greece a few times. Keep it current."

"So..."

He looked so uncertain. Kind of the way he looked when he'd been about to see his sister.

"What happens next?"

She had no idea which question he was asking, a big one or a small one. She picked the easiest to answer.

"I'll buy plane tickets. Get the house aired out. Sylvester will take Granger."

"That's not what I mean."

Her heart stuttered to a near stop. She hadn't moved swift enough to dodge the truth.

"What do you mean?" She did her best airhead actress.

He wasn't biting. His expression remained serious. "With us, Gemma. If I'd walked out today, would you have ever called me again?"

"I just asked you to come to London with me."

"And after that? Are we dating? Are we just fucking? Your builder stud-for-hire? Are we done now that the work is done?"

"Why do you seem angry?" How could he be so cruel? He had to know that he'd stopped being a one-night stand long before that first night. Maybe he was picking a fight to let her down easy. She had to give him an out. "I've just proposed that we take a trip to London. You don't have to say yes. If you want to walk out that door now, you can. I don't want to hold you here, if you don't want to be held here."

Silence stretched for a long moment. Even Granger, who'd nosed his way into the room, stopped sniffing along the floorboards and jumped onto the bed to curl silently by her feet.

Adonis wasn't leaving, pulling on his underwear, slipping into his clothes, but he looked like he was thinking about it. Her heart would be ripped into shreds if he did that.

She needed him. She needed him to know that. It was like an audition. She'd learned long ago that an actress had to care intensely enough that she gave her all and be willing to walk away all at the same time, so the rejection didn't drive her around the bend.

It was time. Taking the deepest breath ever, she pulled her knees up to her chest. It made no sense, what she was doing, but his hands were folded under his arms, where she couldn't reach them, couldn't hold them.

"I love you." She enunciated each word clearly. "I want...us...to be together."

More silence. She looked through the huge window that stretched along the bedroom wall. Stillness met her eyes. Silence filled her ears. It was as if the ocean were on hiatus. Even the wind had paused. *Say something*, she screamed, but only in her head. Taking a cue from Giovanni, she waited.

Finally, finally, he uncrossed his arms and said something.

"When would you want to go?"

It wasn't I love you, but it wasn't goodbye. Her heart sang with the chance that maybe there wa something more on his end, that maybe he needed more time to know that she was sure, strong, determined to make a relationship between them work.

She tucked her feelings away to a corner of her heart and focused on the fact that he wasn't leaving. It wasn't her feelings being reciprocated, but he wasn't leaving. For now, she had to let it be enough.

"Day after tomorrow maybe," she said, her heart scrambling for purchase, but finding nowhere to rest.

"Let's go."

"Are you sure?"

"What's a custard tart?" he asked, and rewarded her with one of his rare million-watt smiles.

She could only take what was offered. It would have to be enough. Then she schooled him on the delights of English desserts.

TWENTY-ONE

Adonis

"I'm so sorry it's pouring on our last day."

"It's fine, Gemma," he said. He knew he was abrupt, but he didn't know how to be kind when their relationship was a speeding train heading toward a certain crash. Every morning he'd woken thinking the trip was either the best or worst idea ever.

"No, it's not. I'm very sorry that I dragged you here. You've hated everything about the last two weeks. You've not said ten words to me for the last ten days. If we weren't shagging every night, I'd think I was living with a ghost. Is it so bad, being with me? Do you hate it that much? I didn't think it was that bad. I don't have a Sylvester here. I don't have any bodyguards. We went to restaurants. I know the purple Bentley saloon is over-the-top, but Sylvester had me pick a car out of a catalog and I liked the Damson."

"Damn what?"

"It's the name of the purple color. Doesn't matter. I told you I love you. And you act like you can barely tolerate being around me. Are you cross because I promised your father I'd arrange everything for his wedding?"

"No. I'm not mad about the wedding or that damned car. You made my father's day when you told him that you'd plan everything."

"Then what's wrong with me? What makes it so hard to be with me?"

She turned to look out the reception room window. When she turned back, something wrenched in his stomach. A single fat tear was coursing down her cheek.

God. He'd hurt her. He'd been so wrapped up in what he thought he was lacking, in what he thought he couldn't give to her, that he'd been blinded to the fact that he was hurting her.

"God, Gemma. I never meant to hurt you. I was giving you space to change your mind."

"Change my mind. About what?"

"About your feelings for me. About you wanting there to be an us."

"You think I'm so fickle that I'd change my mind while we crossed the Atlantic Ocean?"

"I'm your first. I didn't want you imprinting on me like a duckling."

"Why don't you think... Giovanni said that when people talk, they're talking about themselves even if they're saying something different."

He watched her thinking out loud. He wanted nothing

more than for a hole to be torn in the fabric of the universe so he could escape the cold and awful moment when she realized how weak he really was.

"You don't think you deserve love. It's not that you don't believe I can love. You don't believe I can love *you*."

She nailed it. In a couple of minutes, she'd stripped him bare. All the anger and sadness of the last two weeks fell away and it was replaced by pain for how he'd treated her.

He swallowed past the golf-ball-sized lump in his throat. "The last two weeks have been the best of my life. I enjoyed waking up with you, having breakfast with you. Walking the streets of London with you even when it was forty degrees with sleet coming down. I loved shopping with you. I missed you the hours we separated to buy gifts for each other. I was afraid to want you. I was afraid I'd lose you. I was afraid I'd never really had you."

His voice was hoarse as he tried his best to say with all those words, "it's not you it's me." Because it *was* him. He was the damaged one. "I didn't want to be something bad that happened to you. Like I was to the Little family. Like Andy O'Bryan was for you."

"But you're the best thing that ever happened to me. We're not our pasts. We have to be able to define our own futures, otherwise we'd have to give up. I don't want to give up, Adonis. I'm right here. I'm not going anywhere."

"Except back to Los Angeles."

Gemma looked away. Couldn't meet his eyes. Had he been right? California didn't suit her any longer. He'd heard it in every comment she made about being home.

How could they be together if they didn't even have the same definition of home?

"You're not going back to Malibu, are you? You just renovated your house. *I* just renovated your house."

"I'm flying back with you tomorrow. I bought the tickets already. I wouldn't miss Bridget and Dominic's wedding for anything in the world. I'm their wedding planner. That's a promise I won't break."

"But?" He could drive a Mack truck through the gaps in that sentence.

"Jesse introduced me to a producer—"

"You've found a project?" he asked, knowing that despite her words and promises, he was losing her.

"Let me finish. Jesse introduced me to…skip all that backstory. I need to tell this like a movie. Start where the action starts. I've been asked to play Mollie Ralston in *The Mousetrap*."

"In plain English."

"*The Mousetrap*. It's an Agatha Christie story. Murder mystery. Mollie is the inn owner, she's the star of the play."

"That's amazing," he said, lifting her up and twirling her in his arms, thrilled that she wasn't leaving him for London. That a new job was the only secret she'd been harboring. "Congratulations. When do you start? Is this at the theater we visited in Westwood—the Geffen? Or Hollywood? The one downtown?"

"*The Mousetrap* is the longest-running play in London."

"London? This London?" he asked, looking out the window and taking in the hundred and fifty year old buildings that solidified the fact that he wasn't in Malibu or Oxnard or even Los Angeles, but some five thousand miles away—and that he'd been right about all of his assumptions.

"It's been running since nineteen fifty-two," she said, as if that were explanation enough. "I'd have to move to London."

"Have you said yes?"

"I have to give them my decision by tomorrow end of day." She paused for a long time. "I want to do it."

"And you should. Theater would be an amazing challenge for you. Get you out of your comfort zone."

"I just finished renovating my house in Malibu. *You* just finished renovating my house in Malibu," she parroted, a weak attempt at humor.

"It'll keep. I'm sure Sylvester will keep an eye on it for you. Do you want me to stop in?"

She stared at him like he was the creature from the black lagoon. "Stop in?"

"Sure, I—"

A great, gasping sob cut him off.

"Why are you crying? This is super news."

"I wanted you to come with me," she gasped between hiccoughs. "Why do you think I've been doing the hard sell for the last two weeks? I wanted you to love this city as much as I do. To imagine that it could be your home, my home, *our* home."

"To London. To live here?"

"I know you have a business. I know your life is there, your family is there. In my head, in my wildest fantasies, I told you I was offered this job, and you announced that you couldn't live without me, and in some kind of dramatic fashion announced your undying love for me. I don't know. I thought it was going to be like a movie."

He walked from the living room to the back steps. He stomped his way to the kitchen, opening and closing the fridge and cabinets, banging out his frustration. He found matches and lit a fire in the kitchen hearth. It snapped and crackled to life, bringing flickering light and heat to the chilly, damp room.

Eventually, he heard her feet on the steps. "Are you hungry?" She came into the room and closed the open cabinet doors.

"Not for food, Gemma." He stepped away from the fire he'd lit and joined her on the white couch that faced the huge hearth. He pulled her so that her thighs were on top of his.

Had their time here just been a delay of the inevitable?

For a long moment, Gemma looked as though she were screwing up her courage to say something, then, looking like she'd thought better of it, she straddled him fully. Wrapped her arms around his neck and kissed him.

Just like every day of the last two weeks, he could see where this was going, and he wanted her under him, legs wrapped around him, her moaning and crying his name, but something was in the way of his passion.

He pulled back from the kiss, lifted Gemma from his lap and moved to the end of the couch.

"What's wrong?"

"What happens tomorrow?"

"We get to Heathrow, get on the plane, and make the eleven-hour flight back to Los Angeles."

"That's not what I'm getting at, Gemma."

"I'm crap at guessing. I either stay in Malibu and maybe have you, or I come to London and take this dream job. There's no middle ground there. I love you. I want this job. I want you here with me. What do *you* want, Adonis? What will make you happy?"

"This," he said, scooping her up and leading her up the two flights of stairs to her third-floor bedroom of the four-story brick townhouse.

"This," he said, after he'd kissed her until she'd gotten that dazed look in her eye.

"This," he said, while he removed her robe, laid her down on the bed, and kissed every inch of exposed skin until she was writhing, gasping for air.

"This," he said, when he entered her oh so slowly. He controlled his thrusts to maximize her pleasure and minimize the likelihood she was going to come too quickly.

"This," he whispered into her ear when a rosy blush spread out over her breasts, chest, and neck.

"This," he mouthed when he reached down between them and slipped his middle finger against her clitoris, first once, then twice, then a third time, drawing her orgasm from her in gasping sobs.

Only then did he lose his deliberate teasing. Only then did his brain lose its ability to control what came from his mouth.

"I love you, Gemma Hart," he said before he lost all ability to speak, only keeping the ability to feel.

Her blue eyes widened then closed at his words. She bit her lower lip, a sure sign she was on the edge.

"I love you," he said again.

Her breath hitched, and then a low moan escaped as her orgasm rippled through her body. In a minute, he followed.

When he came back from taking care of things, she was quietly tucked under the covers of the antique bed. He slipped into bed, pulled her into his arms, and waited. The normally sunny-yellow room was cast in dark gold shadows. The rain made long streaks along the floor-to-ceiling windows.

He knew better. He knew absolutely one hundred percent better, but he asked the taboo question anyway.

"Did you hear what I said?"

It had been building up for two weeks. Every day they were together, his feelings for her only grew. Cooking with her in the long basement kitchen. Watching what she called quiz shows on her television, promising he could beat her only if he could understand half of what they were saying. He loved her. He'd finally gotten up the courage to tell her. But it wasn't enough to get her to stay in L.A. With every day and every breath, he knew he was losing her to London. He'd never seen her so comfortable, so at home—five thousand plus miles from his own.

"I think we need to pack." She heaved herself from the bed as if the weight of the world was upon her shoulders. After she slipped into her fleece robe, she pulled a suitcase from the closet and started tossing clothes in.

He couldn't be who she wanted. He didn't have a big grand movie gesture in him. To throw down the gauntlet, abandon his family and business, make the big move for love not worrying about the rest. Not now. So, rather than do what he wanted and she needed, he lifted his own suitcase and stacked his sweaters and jeans.

He was a bad story, a tragedy. He didn't get a happy ending.

TWENTY-TWO

Gemma

"How much was all this?" Adonis asked as they walked to the groomed lawn dressed up for a winter wedding, California style.

"The British don't talk about money in polite company. It's my gift to give."

She was happy to have done it. Dominic and Bridget had planned to get married in his backyard or hers when they couldn't find a venue they liked on such short notice. That would have been quaint, cozy, nice even. But Gemma wanted to right a wrong. She'd been so self-involved that she'd let a man lie supine on her floor while she called Sylvester, and Sylvester called his son, and so on.

That had been one of the worst moments of her life. It had also been one of the best moments. It had been a catalyst for change. She'd sought out Giovanni.

She turned toward the man in his dark suit and covered his hand with hers.

"You clean up well."

Adonis threw back his head and laughed. "You make me laugh. Every single day."

"Are you laughing at me, or with me?"

"Both. British people are funny. Will the rest be as funny?"

Gemma purposefully stiffened her upper lip, then put him on the spot. "I don't rightly know. Speaking of London, we can't put this off. I promised to start after the beginning of the year. I need some kind of answer from you. I can't—"

He squeezed her hand. "Later. The happy couple is here."

"Okay. Later." She had to believe in her heart that love would triumph. Wasn't that what this day was all about? Things had been so much better since London. But every night as she lay next to him, watching him sleep, she dreaded the morning, not knowing if he was going to walk out her door, never to return.

Tucking away her anxiety at this being their last time together, at him throwing out the compromise of a long-distance relationship, she plastered on her best smile and went to greet the happy couple.

"I hear you're off to London," Dominic said after kissing her on both cheeks and wrapping her in the world's warmest hug.

"I'm looking forward to it. I only hope I can convince your son to come with me."

"He's gotta hard head, but a big heart. But I know him. He'll make the right decision. Give him time."

Because it was Dominic's wedding, she didn't mention

that she didn't have the luxury of time. In a week's time, she'd be on a whole different continent.

"So, this is Mason Manor…" she started, leading them on a tour of the impressive house that was like a little piece of Britain in Malibu.

After that, she talked to the couple about logistics, food and drink. Leaving them in the small upstairs dressing rooms, she came back down the steps of the stone mansion overlooking the Malibu cliffs and looked at the ocean. As if someone were watching over them, the evening mist didn't come down and shroud the lawn.

She talked to the caterer one last time. An hour later, all was set. The outdoor heaters blazed on the bluff. About thirty white folding chairs were fanned out in an arch facing a trellis draped with winter-white flowers, where the couple would say their vows, but also facing the ocean, where the sun was soon to dip close to the horizon.

On the hill, the house was blazing. Upstairs in dressing rooms, Bridget and Dominic were getting ready. Downstairs, caterers rushed about setting up the reception buffet. Giovanni would be proud. She certainly was.

Gemma crossed her arms, pleased with herself. She'd done good. Finally.

For a moment, the call of seagulls stilled. She looked up into the dusk sky, expecting to see the first stars, but instead was greeted with the whoop-whoop of helicopter blades.

Out of protective instinct, she ducked her head, lifted her skirts and ran toward the house. Out of habit, she lifted her phone and started to dial Sylvester.

"I've got this," Adonis said, laying his hand over the phone.

"I think it's because of me. I'm so sorry. I should have known that booking a house for a wedding would hit the tabloids. I just thought—"

"We've got this."

And they did. Adonis huddled with Nick and Bridget's sons. When they broke it up, Bridget's younger son, Ryan, took out his phone and in ten minutes, the call of birds came back. She almost cried in relief.

Maybe she wouldn't have to go it alone from now on. Maybe she could reach out a hand and ask for help.

Five minutes later, when it was clear the chopper wasn't returning, the music started. Her cheeks widened in a smile she couldn't keep in.

Bruno Mars.

It had seemed kind of a young music choice for the couple, but when she put in a couple of CDs she'd had Sylvester send over, she realized he sang about love and acceptance.

Everyone filed out when "Just the Way You Are" started playing. The seats filled, Bridget's kids in the front row on the left. Zoe and Nick filed down on the right.

"You coming?"

"In a minute," she whispered. She wanted to make sure all was perfect before she took her seat. She ducked into the kitchen and signaled to her surprise.

"Alessandro, I'll never be able to thank you for doing this."

"Who says no when a movie star calls and asks me to

officiate at my younger brother's wedding? Arizona won't miss me while I'm gone."

The man, so much like her lover's father, kissed her and walked outside, making his way to the front. Gasps, hugs, kisses and frantically-whispered conversation filled the air. From what she understood, Dominic's brother hadn't been back to California for a good while.

Dominic came down next. He looked utterly debonair in a navy suit and silver tie. His hair was shiny with product.

"Thanks for this," he said as he leaned down and placed a kiss on her cheek. "Bridget would never indulge and you gave us the excuse to do it up right for her."

"You're welcome. So very welcome."

Alessandro Andreis was looking out at the water, but turned when his brother came to a halt. The men hugged hard for a long time. Gemma swallowed a lump in her throat. She willed herself not to cry.

There was a pause in the music, a moment of quiet as Dominic situated himself under the trellis woven with lilies.

Softly at first, then more loudly, Bruno Mars started again. The first strings of "Marry You" filled the air.

Everyone rose as Bridget appeared on the arm of her eldest son, Cameron. He was in full LAPD dress uniform, white gloves and all. The smile on the older woman's face was tremulous. It was as if Bridget was so happy she wanted to laugh and cry, all at the same time.

Gemma did her best to blink back tears as she smiled at the bride. When the music softened to something instrumental, only then did she take her seat next to Adonis.

"You did good," he whispered in her ear.

"When Sylvester told me that anyone could officiate a wedding, I knew who I had to call."

Alessandro had practiced like he promised and started in the usual way. "We're gathered here today to celebrate the union of my brother, Dominic Andreis, and Bridget Becker. They've prepared their own vows. They've asked that you listen with an open heart and mind."

Alessandro nodded and Dominic turned to the crowd. He pulled a small index card from his breast pocket. He took a deep breath then spoke.

"My life has been long and happy. My greatest lessons, I've learned from my kids. From Nicki, I learned to love with a big heart, and to grab at the unexpected with gusto. From Zoe, I learned that life does have second acts, and that even when you think you can't, you can reinvent yourself. From Adonis, I learned that you have to forgive yourself. Also, the most important, date the hot chick and go with her wherever she asks. You hear me?"

When the laughter died down, Dominic handed Bridget a card.

"What? I don't have pockets in this thing." When she squinted at the words, Dominic took off his reading glasses and slipped them gently onto her nose.

"I guess vanity is one I'm going to have to work on." She turned from her notecard to the small crowd. "Ryan and Cameron, I love you dearly. You've been my life for almost as long as I've been alive. Thank you for all you've done, but

I think this guy can take it from here. I've learned a lot from the two of you. How to mend furniture. How to stop a fight. Seriously though, Ryan, from you, I've learned to expect the unexpected, and be okay with it. From Cameron, and you too, Yesenia, I've learned that life is about grabbing at the second chance for happiness. I promise, Dominic, to hold tight to our second chance with both hands."

Alessandro smiled at his brother again and nodded.

"I love California in all its hippy-dippy greatness. But I'm a traditional guy. I, Dominic, take you, Bridget, to be my wife, to have and to hold from this day forward, for better, for worse, for richer, for poorer, in sickness and in health, to love and to cherish, until we are parted by death.

"This is my solemn vow."

If Gemma thought she could hold back tears during Dominic's love letter to his children, then it was doubly hard now. She'd never been in a place with so much love. She swallowed hard. Then it was Bridget's turn.

Bridget repeated the same vows, nearly word for word. The couple looked at each other as if the rest of the world had fallen away. As if it was just the two of them.

Suddenly, achingly, she wanted this. This joining of lives, this joining of souls. She looked down between her and Adonis and grabbed his hand and squeezed, hoping he got the implicit message there.

"By the power vested in me, by the State of California, for one day only, I pronounce you man and wife. You may kiss the bride."

If she thought this older couple would skip that part, she was dead wrong. Her throat clogged and she had to look away. If anyone asked, she'd blame the tears on the setting sun.

"I present to you, Dominic and Bridget Andreis."

Gemma was out of her seat the moment the couple started the recession.

"Congratulations." She shook the hands of the new couple, kissed both of them, then escaped to the reception area.

She pulled the manager aside. "I need a minute. Where can I go?"

"There's a little room on the third floor," he said, not skipping a beat. "Do you — "

"I'll find it," she said, lifting her skirt and running from the room.

What people don't tell you about being a recluse is that it's easy. No messy relationships, sex, or emotions get in the way when you're alone. She needed that solitude just now. Giovanni's advice had seemed so innocent. Go out. Meet people. Make friends.

Then she'd fallen in love.

All the feels. That's what Americans said now. All the feels. She had them. Love for this little family she'd adopted. Love for Adonis. Fear for the future and all she couldn't control.

When a knock sounded on the door, she ducked into the tiny powder room. Pulling square after square of toilet paper from the roll, she dabbed at her eyes, blew her nose.

"Hello," she said to Adonis, who was sitting on a tiny Queen Anne chair at an equally tiny vanity.

"What happened?"

"Overwhelmed is all. We better get back down there. You have to make a toast, right? You and Cameron."

"No one's going anywhere. Let them get a couple of drinks."

"I got sparkling grape juice for you."

"I'm sure you've got it covered, Gemma. You're an excellent planner."

"This was a walk in the park. You should see a movie director pull together a two-hour feature."

Zoe's head poked into the room. "They're about to start the toast... Oh, you know what. We'll wait." The door slammed and Gemma could hear her murmuring to someone else, then high heels descended the narrow stairs.

"Oh, Gemma. My life was like a bad movie, that started with a tragedy and the guy lived like a zombie. Dad was right in what he said today. Life is about second acts and second chances. Yes, I'll go to London with you. I'm going to grab on to you with both hands and never let go. If that's okay with you."

"I love you, Adonis Andreis," she said, free for the first time to love him and all his flaws, knowing that he loved her and all of hers.

"I'll love you forever, Gemma Hart." Adonis sank to one knee, and produced his own notecard from his pocket.

"I'm confused."

"I was going to do this downstairs. And yes, I got my father's permission. It was partially his idea. But now's the right time. Here goes.

"Gemma Wynter Hart, I love you. I promise to take the second chance that life has given us. I promise to keep your house in order, love your dog like he was my own, and pamper you all the days of my life. Gemma Hart, will you marry me?"

"Yes! Of course. Yes."

"I think we need to get down for the toasts."

"Right. Yes. Let's chivvy along."

"I vow to get a teacher and learn British English. Starting with spanners. I'm thinking I'm going to need a lot of those."

Gemma dabbed her eyes, swatted him with her free hand then pulled him down the stairs to start their future.

ABOUT THE AUTHOR

JOLIE MOORE

Crazy Beautiful Love

I write crazy, beautiful love stories because I believe story-telling is magic. I love complicated heroines with secrets, strong heroes who fall hard, and a long winding road to happily ever after. When I'm not writing, I love to travel to witness the diverse tapestry of humanity, photograph the beauty of the world, visit museums, and watch live theater. I live in West Hollywood, California ten miles from the nearest airport.

♥

I'm the host of Fifty First Dates the Podcast. I haven't found my own happily ever after, but I'm not done look-ing. Join me as I try to find my Mr. Right or maybe Mr.

Right Now in Southern California. #50firstdates
#joliemoore #crazybeautifullove